Alex Campbell

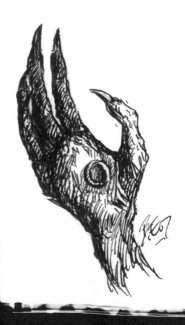

LYE STREET

LYE STREET

A novella of the Deepgate Codex

ALAN CAMPBELL

SUBTERRANEAN PRESS ⊰⊱ 2008

First Edition

ISBN
978-1-59606-135-4

Subterranean Press
PO Box 190106
Burton, MI 48519

www.subterraneanpress.com

IN THE YEAR 511, Henry Bucklestrappe set fire to the townhouses on Morning Road in the district of Applecross, to rid the street, he said, of the demonic messages which had been appearing on their walls. He was apprehended, but not before the flames wreaked havoc. Few of the buildings could be saved. The Spine removed Bucklestrappe to a cell for punishment, but he did not die there.

He was murdered a year later, exactly as the messages had predicted. No one could fathom how he had been extracted from the temple dungeons, yet his corpse was discovered half a league away, stuffed into a cistern in Callow. Deepgate's priests refused to bless the corpse in the Church of Ulcis, so Bucklestrappe's sons took it to the Deadsands, where they left it to be eaten by crows.

For a while, the messages stopped appearing.

Then, almost fifty years later in the winter of 561, people in Lilley woke to find that the whitewashed archway on the southern side of the Swan Bridge had been defaced. Someone had scrawled this:

Buckle strapp of Applecross. Killed in 562.

Beneath the text was a rude picture of a knife, almost child-like in its simplicity. The locals painted over it that same day, but they could not whitewash the gossip. Rumours spread out and inevitably reached the ears of poor Henry's sons. One of them, a butcher by trade, left Deepgate with his family to start a new life in Sanpah. The other son was Norman Bucklestrappe. He had invested a considerable fortune in the city construction projects, and so, he elected to stay. He begged the priests for refuge in the temple, but was refused.

The Spine pulled his corpse from a pipe six months later. His murderer had broken all of his bones and removed the blood from his veins.

For another fifty years, the messages ceased.

By 612, the murders had been forgotten by most folks. Only Nellie Cripp, old Henry's granddaughter remembered the curse, but she had married and so given up her doomed family name (if not the house and pearls). She believed herself to be immune. The priests did not connect her violent murder to a message sketched in charcoal across a chimneypot nearby, in which the nature and date of Mrs Cripp's demise had been accurately noted.

They had assumed the note to be a memorial, of sorts, written *after* the fact.

They were wrong.

ONE NIGHT IN THE AUTUMN of 1012, an angel climbed into an attic in Gardenhowe. She had been searching for a dark corner to hide from temple assassins, but what she found was a note scrawled across a large section of pulpboard.

Learn the TRUTH! Go to the tower in Lye Street.

Underneath this, someone had sketched a rude picture of a knife with a circle in the hilt, very much like the one she always carried with her. Carnival stared hard at the drawing, suspecting a trap. The message looked old, and had been stained by years of grime and bat guano, yet there was something oddly disturbing about the handwriting. Its tone and fervour made her feel uncomfortable. She decided to find another hideaway, and she vowed to avoid the tower in Lye Street.

She climbed up through the rafters and out through the ragged hole she'd found in the roof. She ran lightly across the lead flashings, and then, reaching the edge of the building, spread out her wings and leapt into the night sky.

Deepgate spun below her as she banked, the vast foundation chains turning around her like the spokes of an enormous wheel.

Townhouses and bridges crowded around the temple, their old stonework dappled yellow where oil lanterns glowed. She flew out across the Warrens, that maze of chimneypots and gutters, all dark now but for a few lamplighters heading back from the temple districts. The wind lifted her high, up towards the half-moon and the stars. She breathed cool air, still fresh with the scent of recent rain, and gazed down at her city.

Spine crawled like lice over the rooftops. From this height she could not distinguish between the black leather armour of the Cutters and the Adepts. But the temple assassins were all armed and trained to look for shadows in the sky. They would be watching for her silhouette against the stars.

Carnival lifted her knees and dove. Her scarred hands flashed in the moonlight. Her long black hair streamed behind her ears. She threw herself into the dive, picking up speed, then looped around a column of factory smoke, and levelled her descent. A crooked lane zigzagged beneath her, the tenements weaving back and forth. She dipped under a cross-chain, then over another. Then she pulled back hard, thumping her wings, and settled on the upper storey of a partially built house-bridge.

It was one of many such constructions underway. Carnival glanced at the freshly painted street signs on either side of the abyssal gap. The house-bridge spanned a canal of empty air, connecting the new Chapelfunnel coalgas plants to a rut of labourers' tenements in Gardenhowe. The walls on this level had been built to chest height and already pinned to the foundation chains below. Yet the project had evidently halted months ago. The tarpaulins had blown clean off and now hung over the edge, leaving the warped timber floor exposed to the elements. Shutters had yet to be installed in the lower level, which meant it would be considered uninhabitable and deserted at night. As good a place as any to hide for a while. She squeezed through a square opening in the floor and let herself drop.

Down here, only the dimmest glimmer of moonlight permeated the darkness, but Carnival's night eyes were accustomed to gloom. She found two chairs used to prop up timbers for sawing, dragged one aside and sat down. Then she blinked.

Someone had scrawled a message across the plastered wall.

Make haste! Go to the tower in Lye Street!

Below this was a sketch of a knife, very much like the one Carnival always carried.

AT THE END OF THAT AUTUMN, an old prospector named Sal Greene went to visit a colleague of his, a scoundrel and self-proclaimed occultist who lived in a private suite above the Phantasmacists Club in Ivygarths.

"Ten twelve, Laccus, is swiftly running out."

"Ah, yes," said the other man, closing the door behind his guest. "The year you bleed to death, Sal?"

"Not if you can help it."

Greene was grey-haired now, with black veins pushing out of the backs of his hands, but under his tatty woollen topcoat he remained the same powerful man who'd swung a pick axe in Hollowhill back in the seventies.

He hung the coat on a stand, then halted when he saw the grisly display Laccus Ravencrag had arranged for his benefit. "What sort of fucking barbarism is this?" he said gruffly.

"What? Oh, you mean the dead dogs?"

"Aye, the dead dogs."

The phantasmacist had nailed three dogs to a plank of wood, one above the other, and then linked the bodies together with all manner of rubber tubes, wires and metal struts. One of the tubes dripped blood into a jar.

"Magic, is it?"

"You know me, Sal."

"And what does all this colourful surgery accomplish?"

Ravencrag coughed a wedge of phlegm into his cheek then chewed it. "Summons the demon I told you about," he said. "Sit down, Sal. I reckon I just saved your life."

The prospector eased himself into a big leather chair and waited to be convinced or repulsed and angered enough to beat this crooked little schemer out of his skin for wasting precious time. Any one of the outcomes suited him at the moment. Laccus Ravencrag had a ticking clock on the wall, and Greene didn't much care for the smell of corpses.

"When the hounds died," said Laccus, "they all made different sounds. That's death chatter, you see?"

Greene frowned. "I'm not moved, Laccus."

"See this one." The phantasmacist peeled the skin back from the skull of a dog and showed the gleaming bone by the light of his tallow candle. The cranium was etched with criss-cross scars. "You see the markings?"

"You cut those in?" asked Greene.

"I cut them in," agreed Laccus. "That's Azzarat's summoning script. Now watch the jar at the end."

Greene saw something shift in the red fluid. "What you put in there? Newts?"

"Maggots. And I didn't put them there. They grew from nothing."

The prospector peered closer. "You're saying you got one of your spells to work at last? Just when we need it to, at the eleventh fucking hour? Forgive me, Laccus, but I think you put the maggots in the jar yourself. What's more, I reckon you're diddling me. Anyone would think you wanted to clean me out in my final days."

"Watch them for a while, Sal, before you make up your mind. You'll have a drink?"

"Have you poisoned it?"

"Heavily."

"Why the Hell not, then? What do I have to lose?"

They drank and, to Greene's actual surprise, Laccus Ravencrag had not poisoned the whisky. The prospector got healthily drunk, and watched the maggots closely as he'd been asked to. They were black, shadowy little things, eerie and unnatural looking. They seemed to appear and disappear like shadows under fast moving clouds. The two men talked some more, and in time Greene came to understand the significance of the spell.

"You're making worm ghosts, Laccus."

"I am."

"Ghosts," said Greene, "in a jar."

"All wriggling around like the grimoire said they would," said Ravencrag. "I've been watching them for days now. They've been getting more excited as the demon gets close. He's coming to hear you out, old man, just like I promised he would."

For once Greene chose to believe the phantasmacist: Laccus fucking Ravencrag, the man they said had flung his own wife into the abyss; the man who, in his declining years, had turned his fetish for the grotesque to the study of apparitions. *The Phantasmacists Club?* Of late Greene had come to think of them as a bunch of idiots with jinnee bottles and queer, pudding-bowl hats. Not one of them had come close to solving the problem until now. Yet looking at the worms in the jar of blood, the prospector felt a twinge of hope. The maggots were the strangest looking things he'd seen in a long while.

He shook his head in astonishment. "The last grimoire worked? You know how much that cost?"

"Tuppence, I seem to recall you saying."

"How come that one worked when all the costly ones failed?"

"You were robbed on the costly ones, Sal."

"So you'll be handing them back to me?"

"Not this winter," the phantasmacist said. "I need something to keep my fire going." He grinned under his odd little hat. "You paid me to test the spell, and that's what I've done. Judging by the maggots, Basilis will be here any day soon."

That soon? "What? He's got wings?"

"Did have once, or so the grimoire says."

The prospector blew through his teeth. He felt relieved, and not only because he'd not been poisoned by a dose of dogweed in the booze. But he was becoming concerned too. Ravencrag's apparent success meant that Greene would owe two fists of virgins' gall stones to the demon for his summoning fee, which was a problem now that he came to think about it.

"You'd better pay him," said Ravencrag, as though he'd the read the other man's mind. "Or you're dead." He poured himself another shot of whisky. "Worse than dead, in fact. Ayen's one powerful, spiteful bitch. Imagine what her hired killers are like." He waved his glass at Greene. "Then imagine what the hired killers she kicks out of Heaven are like, the ones strong enough and dangerous enough to try to fuck her over. Oh, Basilis supported the god of chains when it suited him, but do you see him grovelling at the feet of our Lord now? Nope. He betrayed Ulcis as soon as the coup failed, and wandered off into the wilds, leaving the god of chains trapped down there in the abyss. This bastard doesn't care how many gods he pisses off. Trust me, Sal, you don't want to mess with someone like that."

"Don't you worry about the demon's fee," said Greene, raising his glass. "I got that all ready."

Where the Hell was he going to find two fists of virgins' gall stones? Did he even *know* any virgins?

"And don't you try to cheat me," Ravencrag added. "I want my bonus the moment the sod gets here."

"Aw…I was just going to have you murdered, Laccus. Save myself some gold."

"That would be funny if I didn't believe you." Nevertheless Ravencrag showed a mouth of yellow teeth. "I spent thirty years learning about ghosts," he said with pride. "And another five avoiding harm from them. You know how you get shades appearing after you spill a tinker's guts? That got me thinking. I mean, why would Hell come sniffing round a tinker's corpse? What use are those fuckers going to be in the Maze? What they going to beg for?" His laugh sounded like a pig snort. "Souls are worthless, Sal. Even scum have the fucking things."

He leaned forward, conspiratorial like, and stinking of whisky. "But I knew *he* would come when *I* summoned him, and I wanted to prove it to you, Sal. I respect you for standing your ground here in Deepgate. Folks like you and me have better souls than half the shit in this city. We matter."

This admission was, Greene reckoned, intended to be a compliment. His fist relaxed on the glass.

"That's why you're sitting here all rubbery with drink," Ravencrag went on, "and not crowded into the back of an ox carriage bound for Sanpah." His long hooked nose dipped like a well pump. "Most men would have fled when they read Mack's letter, taken their fortunes and quit the city."

Greene remembered his old man's letter, delivered by a suit from the firm of Messrs Hooke and Highfield.

Dear Son,

If you're reading this then it's 1012 and I've been dead for 50 years. I hope you've had a good life in our Holy City, and that you stayed away from heathens like I told you to, and found God in the end. And I hope your life's been free of worry, because that's all about to change. Our family is cursed...

He'd gone on to describe the scarred angel's vendetta against the descendants of Henry Bucklestrappe, and how he would pray to Ulcis to keep them all safe.

Trust in the god of chains, son. The faithful will prevail.

Yet, the letter proved that Mack Greene had had reservations. He'd left strict instructions with the family solicitors not to deliver his warning before 1012, the very year his son was due succumb to the curse. He hadn't done this to hide the awful truth and so spare Sal fifty years of worry. No, he'd done this because he'd been a bastard. Had Greene known of the family curse fifty years ago, he'd have sold the house and disappeared across the Deadsands, spending his fortunes wisely, in gin dens and brothels.

But then Mack Greene had always disapproved of his son's godless, wandering nature. This was the old man's way of reprimanding Sal from the grave.

The prospector grumbled, "I don't run from my troubles any more, Laccus. I'm too old for that nonsense now."

"Here's to dead angels." Ravencrag clinked glasses then raised his own and hallooed like a priest at the Sinner's Well gallows. "Every fifty years! How the *fuck* does she remember? Your great-great-granddaddy must have seriously pissed her off."

"He had that way with women. Much like yourself."

The phantasmacist grinned.

"But what if the demon doesn't agree to help," said Greene, who had begun to feel wheezy and uncertain. *Two fists of virgins' gall stones?* "I mean, what if he doesn't want to kill an angel?"

"Hmm…" Ravencrag looked thoroughly unconcerned. "Then he'll probably just slit your throat and stuff your soul in a bottle of wasps. Torture it for all eternity, that sort of thing."

"Nothing too bad, then?"

"Nah. I wouldn't worry about it." He took another sip. "Come to think of it, I don't worry about it. I think we should talk about my bonus now."

Ravencrag could stuff his bonus up his arse. He wasn't getting a penny of it. Spooky maggots notwithstanding, the phantasmacist had no real power. But the demon? Now that was a whole different level of nastiness. Two whole *fists* of gall stones? Removed from virgins? In *this* city? Greene wondered if Ayen's former cutthroat would accept two fists of spinsters' teeth. He might, at least, be able to purchase those from the Heshette. The prospector's supposed wealth had been a carefully constructed web of lies. He had the house on Lye Street, of course, yet he'd nothing but cobwebs left in his coffers. Ravencrag and his penchant for bloody grimoires had eaten the rest of it over the last few months. Greene had probably financed the Phantasmacists Club out of his own pocket.

His daughter Ellie and her husband Jack would receive a poor inheritance, he feared. Yet he'd done everything he could to ensue they wouldn't be burdened with the angel's curse. They were happy here in Deepgate. And that, after all, was the main reason he'd stayed in the chained city himself.

Tortured in a bottle of wasps for all eternity?

The prospector sighed.

The things I do to keep my family safe.

I T WAS DUSK WHEN the ox carriage reached the chained
city. In the west, only a red ribbon remained of the departing
day, like a forest fire raging across the horizon. The air above the
abyss rim remained cool and fresh, heavy with the smell of wet
metal and rust.

The beasts snorted and steamed as the vehicle rumbled to a
halt behind them, its yellow wooden slats bright in the sunset.
It had halted close to the edge of the precipice, in what appeared
to be a deserted settlement of adobe huts, all shadowed by great
hummocks of stone, logs, slate and lime. The carriage door
creaked open and a man hopped down. He strolled to the lip
of the chasm, to where a broad wooden rope bridge dipped
away into the city. He was of average height and weight, but
with clear, quick eyes and an energetic gait. A tall black hat sat
at a jaunty angle upon his head, and he wore an ancient red
leather topcoat full of numerous pockets, heavily patched and
patterned with black wire filigree, feathers and teeth. In one fist
he clutched a walking stick (a gut-sticker, disguised) which he
dug into the bridge planks to measure their strength and degree
of decay.

The greasy wood crumbled under the point of his stick.
"Rotten," he called back to the coachman.

"Just as I said, Sir," the coachman replied from his high sprung seat at the front of the carriage. "The main route down to the temple won't be finished for months, and that woodway's not strong enough for oxen and carts. If you don't mind, I'll have to drop you here."

Othniel Cope gave the man a curt nod, then turned back to admire the view. "This is fine," he said.

Deepgate spread out below him, a vast metal web suspended over the mouth of the abyss. Anchors driven into the bedrock around the abyss perimeter supported the weight of the chains, yet despite their girth and strength, the city sagged towards the centre, like a bowl of ironwork full of dismal stone dwellings. Only the Church of Ulcis rose to any great height. Yet the great building still appeared to be under construction, its black spires and turrets clad in scaffolding.

Cope pointed with his stick. "When will the temple be complete?"

"Another ten years, Sir," the coachman replied. "But they've being saying that for the last five hundred years. I doubt we'll see the Rookery Spire finished in our lifetimes."

"Not in your lifetime, at any rate," muttered Cope.

The coachman turned on his seat and began to unstrap his passenger's travel bag from the roof of the carriage.

Building work appeared to be underway throughout most of Deepgate. A mass of townhouses clustered around the temple, all interwoven with arched bridges and chains, yet further out the structures thinned to a clutter of timber shacks and hemp cords. Stanchions held ropes, pulleys and bucket lifts—evidently for moving materials and equipment—while slender walkways dipped, rose and zigzagged through it all, like drapes of lace.

One of these walkways climbed, by way of a series of beams and platforms, in a crooked line from the centre of the city up to the lip of the abyss before them. It was wide enough for two oxen to walk abreast, though it looked perilously fragile and steep in places. "Has something delayed the construction of these hanging roads?" asked Cope.

The coachman untied knots around the luggage. "The workers are waiting on more sapperbane," he said, "but the Tooth won't be back from Blackthrone for another week. Once we get some decent cross-chains down there, we'll be able to bring beasts down into the Warrens." He tugged at a clasp. "Stone and timber has to be bucket-lifted or manhandled down a block at a time for fear of collapsing the woodways, and we keep losing ropes, pulleys and timber to the bloody tinkers."

"Tinkers?"

The other man grunted. "They live in those shacks on the fringes." He freed Cope's travel bag and handed it down to him, before returning to loosen the straps around his own luggage—bales of some foul-smelling animal skins, from what Cope could gather.

"Most of the new immigrants don't have a penny," the coachman went on. "Beggars and cut-purses coming in from the

river towns. Scroungers, the lot of them. We put up woodways…
they strip them for pulpboard and hemp, or steal what they can
from the labourer's camps around the abyss. Then they build
their own hovels on any bit of chain going free down there. No
permissions, no planning, just leagues of rope. Half the Holy
City is a slum."

"The Church does not object?"

The coachman shrugged. "Presbyter Scrimlock's been trying
to get them all recorded on the census. But there's so many of
the blighters." He heaved one bale over the luggage rack and
let it fall to the ground, and then started untying another.
"All crawling around in the nets under the Warrens, looking
for rubbish that's fallen from the streets above." He shook his
head. "Even the children are at it, gangs of them. What kind of
man would let his young ones crawl around in those nets, eh?
Thieving little shits, just like their parents. They take what they
want. It's not right when the rest of us are forced to pay so much
for everything."

"Not even your refuse is safe from theft?"

"Principle of the thing, Sir."

Cope withdrew a silver watch from his one of his many
pockets and glanced at it. "You have arrived precisely on time,
despite the floods, and so you have earned the truppenny bonus
I promised."

"Very kind of you, sir." He hefted a second bale over the
side of the carriage. "Sir?"

"Yes?"

"Forgive me, but…" He hesitated. "…the folks in Sanpah
know you. They say you're a thaumaturge, that you can work
magic." He glanced down at Cope, then quickly away again. "I
was wondering if I could ask you a question?"

"By all means."

The coachman gestured towards the abyss. "What's really down there?" he asked. "I mean, the Church says this, and the heathens say that. I believe the Church, don't get me wrong, it's just that…"

"You can't be certain."

"Aye."

"And you'd like to know for sure."

"I would, sir. It seems to me that we're putting so much effort into building the city…and we're paying so much tax for it and all…"

"And you want to be sure your investment is sound?"

"Investment?" The man grinned. "That's it exactly, Sir."

"Glad to help," said Cope. He pulled his gut-sticker free from its walking stick sheathe and buried the thin metal spike in the nearest ox's rump. The beast bellowed and bulled against its harness and, kicking out with its back legs, struck the underside of the driver's seat. The coachman lost his balance and fell across the leather cushions. Cope drove his gut-sticker deeper into the ox's flesh.

The animal bolted.

The carriage leapt forward. Dragged by the panicking beasts, the heavy vehicle clattered onto the walkway. Hemp ropes stretched under its weight. Planks dipped, buckled, and split beneath its wheels. The carriage slewed to one side, buckling the walkway. One of the rear wheels slipped off the edge. The axle hit the deck, then chewed through dozens of boards as the oxen continued to drag their burden forward. Both animals grunted and stamped and scrabbled to find purchase on the planks. But the carriage weighed too much. It slid off the walkway, taking the harness, oxen, and coachman with it.

Cope watched the vehicle plummet fifty feet before it struck a foundation chain and burst apart. The driver and his animals slipped between the chains, disappearing into the dark abyss below. For a long moment, the surviving ropes all quivered.

The thaumaturge withdrew a tiny ragged dog from one of his topcoat's inner pockets, then held it up close to his face. "Happy now, Basilis?" he said.

The pup growled.

"Such a simple question to answer," muttered Cope. "Still, I've saved us a truppenny."

Cope returned the tiny dog to his pocket, picked up his travel bag, and set off down the walkway, cautiously for it had been badly damaged.

THE QUEER MESSAGES BEGAN to appear everywhere Carnival went, always one step ahead of her movements, as if their author had intimate knowledge of the dark and derelict places she frequented. In a basement of a pendulum house Ivygarths:

The **TRUTH** lies in **LY** e **STREET**.

In an attic in Lilley:

Re**D**eem your self, **BITCH!** The tower in **LYE**.

The words became increasingly hostile and accusatory, the charcoal lines more savagely scrawled on brick or plaster. And always, beneath each note was a drawing of the knife Carnival carried. Each time she found another note, her terror grew. She thought she knew who was writing them.

Her nightly flights through the city became desperate hunts for a place where she could hide, not only from the Spine, but from these written demands. The worst messages stirred deep memories, like flashes from forgotten dreams, which she battled to contain.

In an upper room of a tall flint townhouse, a place full of ticking clocks, she found an old woman who had died in her bed and been partially eaten by a pack of blue-eyed cats. The creatures sat on furniture, purring softly, and watched the angel. All three of the dressing table mirrors had been smashed. Words had been cut into the wallpaper with a knife.

BEWARE A CAGe hidden. Lye Street.

MURDERER.

WHITTENWHITTENWHT. LYE STREET.

Carnival squeezed her hands over her ears, as if to block out screaming, and fled across the moonlit rooftops. She abandoned one hideaway and then another, and then, when she could not think of another place to go, she fought her hideous fear of the abyss and dove between the chains of Gardenhowe.

Iron foundations loomed over her head, immense and black and scabbed with rust. The vast darkness below the district groaned under the weight of sixty thousand homes, and seemed to compress the blood in her muscles. On she crawled, through girders, pipes and filth. Welds cut her wings and hands, scratched her old leather vest and breeches, but she didn't slow. She scrambled through fallen detritus snagged in a hemp net, through broken furniture, booze bottles and tin cans, pigeon shit and rotting clothes.

Rust had eaten through the side of an underfloor rain cistern, forming a jagged hole. The angel folded her wings tightly against her back and climbed inside the tank. It stank of old water. Her hands moved through slime. Crouched, she rested her wings against the wall and closed her eyes.

She heard the city shifting above her, the cooling metal and grousing chains, and she could almost imagine echoes answering from the great abyss below, deep mournful sounds like the cries of gods. She shivered, and opened her eyes.

Scratched into the rust before her was another message. It was faint, but Carnival read it easily.

Listen to the corpse in LYE STREET.

The angel heard screaming, close to her own ears. It sounded like the shrieks of a madwoman.

S AL GREENE AWOKE in his chair before the fire. His daughter was standing beside him in her crumpled nightdress, shaking his shoulder. She looked sleepy. "Father," she said. "Did you not hear the ruckus? He was banging on the door loud enough to wake the street."

"Ellie?" The prospector rubbed his eyes. "What's wrong?" His first thought was that another Dalamoorish assassin had arrived at his door with a babe in a basket, but his panic subsided when he saw the note in her hand.

"A lad brought this for you." She handed him the folded scrap of paper and scowled. "It's from Mr Ravencrag."

"When did this arrive?"

"Just now."

Greene picked up his reading glass from the mantel and squinted through it. It was the summons he'd been waiting for. His excitement grew. "What time is it?"

"After two."

"Gods balls," he muttered. "I must have dozed off. Sorry you were disturbed, princess. How's Mina?"

"That one could sleep through a war." Ellie gave him a weary smile. "She's as bad as you."

Greene returned his daughter's smile. Sometimes Ellie

reminded him of his poor sister Margaret, who had been killed by the hooking cough when they'd both been young, and sometimes, like now, she was the image of the Dalamoor Princess he most suspected to be her mother, although he could not remember that woman's name. He'd been blind drunk at the time and the Vizier had had nine daughters. A year had passed before the sallow-skinned knifeman had turned up at his house in Deepgate, carrying Ellie in his arms, and a curt note from the Vizier in which the word 'bastard' had been used in several different, but colourful ways.

He took his daughter's hand and gave it a squeeze. "Did Jack wake?"

"No."

"Good, he needs his rest."

Jack had moved into the house after he'd married Ellie. Greene had always felt a twinge of guilt that he hadn't been able to help them more. A young couple ought to have their own home. However, the townhouses in Ivygarths and Lilley were far beyond his means. Jack's job as a skilled woodworker entitled him to a place in one of the Workers' Shares in Dourbridge, but if they had to live in the Warrens, then wasn't it better to be here with him than crammed into a lower tenement with four other families? Besides, Greene liked having his family around, especially little Mina.

"I don't like Mr Ravencrag," said Ellie. "The things people say about him. I don't trust him."

"I don't trust him either," Greene gave her a kiss on the cheek, "which is why I spend so much time down there. Get back to bed now, lass."

Presbyter Scrimlock's lackeys had not yet seen fit to proclaim Lye Street safe for carts, oxen and camels, so Greene was forced to walk all the way from his house to the Phantasmacists Club in Ivygarths. Despite his woollen gloves, the cold night air stole into his hands and gnawed at his arthritic joints. The pain had worsened these last few years. Often he wondered if a speck of isinglass or quartz had become trapped in his knuckles, some fragment from a mine he'd once looted. Still, he thanked the Gods that he was mobile. Unlike Ravencrag with his weak hip, Greene could hurry when he felt inclined to, as he felt inclined to now.

He was going to meet a demon.

Ravencrag, when he opened the door to his private rooms, wore a dark expression on his hawkish face. "There's no pissing demon," he hissed. "Just some sprat *claiming* to be his representative. Frankly, I'm not impressed."

Greene pushed past and immediately saw the cause of his colleague's doubts. The man could not have been more than twenty years old: foppish and handsome, but with an arrogant twist to his lips. He wore a red leather topcoat festooned with pockets, yet extravagantly patterned with black wire and tribal fetishes, and he carried a walking stick, topped with pommel made from animal teeth. Clear blue eyes studied Greene from beneath the brim of a tall black set at such an angle that it appeared to be in danger of falling from his head.

"Who the Hell are you?" asked Greene.

The young man extended a hand. "Othniel Cope, at you service."

"Sal Greene." He accepted the hand; it was soft and damp.

"My master heard your summons," said Cope.

The accent sounded odd. The prospector could not place it. "Your master?"

"The demon Basilis. I am his intermediary, Mr Greene. Since his fall from Heaven, Basilis has used one thaumaturge or another to speak on his behalf."

A thaumaturge? No wonder Ravencrag was in such a foul mood. The phantasmacist had no patience for practitioners of rival arts.

Ravencrag hobbled over. The cold weather had evidently aggravated his hip. He squeezed past the plank of dead dogs, and then eased himself down in to the seat closest to the stove. With his crooked shoulders all hunched over, and his hooked nose poking out from the folds of his topcoat, he looked more like a gargoyle than usual.

Greene and Cope joined him around a table.

"You are wondering," Cope said to Greene, "if I am who I claim to be."

"Well…" The prospector had been thinking exactly that.

"How could a man of my apparent youth be the guardian of Ayen's Hounds, the skulls described by Azzarat the Nomad in his grand grimoire? You have a copy of the Heshette tome, I see." He pointed his walking stick at Ravencrag's ghoulish gallows.

"We have the book," Greene said. He thought it best not to tell Cope how little he'd paid for it. After Ravencrag had eliminated the rare and expensive magic tomes, they moved on to the common editions, followed by the cheap ones, and then finally the tat the heathens sold at Sanpah flea market. *The Book of the Hound* was into its fortieth ragged edition and propped up many tables north of Clune.

Cope lowered his walking stick and then twirled it between his hands. "Basilis grants his servants longevity," he said, "for as long as it pleases him to do so. I have served my master faithfully now for one hundred and sixty three years, during which time I have not once failed him. In return, I am permitted to retain my youth."

"What happens if you make a mistake?"

"I do not make mistakes, Mr Greene." The thaumaturge smiled thinly, then set down his walking stick. "My master's fee will be two fists of gall stones," he said. "Each one must have been removed from the body of a virgin. Basilis finds such morsels quite delicious." He paused, staring hard at the other man. "Of course, if you cannot procure these delicacies, your own soul will be an acceptable alternative."

"You'll have your stones, after you do your job."

"And what is the job?"

The prospector hesitated.

"He wants you to kill a fucking angel," said Ravencrag.

Cope arched his thin dark eyebrows. "I see." He placed his tall hat on the floor beside his travel bag. Then, from one of the many inner pockets of his topcoat, he brought out a tiny dog. A thin, mangy creature no larger than his hand, it appeared to be suffering from some painful malady. Patches of fur had fallen out, revealing scabrous grey skin. Its ears were leathery and ragged, as though they had been chewed by older and larger pups. A repulsive crust had form at the corners of its eyes, which it seemed unable to open.

The thaumaturge held up the tiny creature. "Let me introduce my master, Gentlemen," he said. "This is the demon Basilis, formerly Ayen's Hound Master and Heaven's Lord of Warfare. It is from him that you must beg aid."

The dog gave a low, pitiful wail.

Greene failed to stifle a guffaw. "This pup is a demon?"

Cope nodded.

Ravencrag spat on his own floor. He peered out from under his pudding bowl hat, studying the dog with undisguised contempt. Finally he said, "I've seen scabbier mutts than that one," he said. "But not many. Do you want to kick this charlatan out now, Greene? Or should we rob the bastard first?"

"Gentlemen!" Cope's tone demanded no further frivolity. He raised his free hand. "Do not let his humble appearance fool you. The Hound Master's physical form was destroyed in the War Amongst the Gods. Ayen condemned his soul by trapping it in this animal. In this form, Basilis cannot wield his power on earth. Nor can he die."

The pup growled.

"An impotent demon," said Ravencrag. "It's original, I'll give you that, Cope. Funny how that prick Azzarat never mentioned this in his cheap and wildly distributed sales pitch. What's his share of the con?"

The thaumaturge's expression darkened. His eyes thinned and his lips twisted into a cruel and dangerous smile. Suddenly he looked much older than his apparent years. "You are the amateur here," he said in an ominously low voice. "Do not mock me, Sir."

Ravencrag scowled and chewed his lip. For a moment Greene thought he would respond, but thankfully the phantasmacist said nothing more.

Cope unbuttoned his travel bag and drew back the flap. It was full of bones, and three long-jawed skulls: of hounds or foxes. He withdrew one these and set it on the table beside the pup. The relic was old and yellowed, about a foot long and brimming with sharp teeth. The top of the cranium hinged back to reveal a hollow where the brain had once been. This was full of dust. "If you wish to beg my master's aid," he said, "you must first allow him to gaze upon you. I require a drop of blood from each of you, to add to this powder."

"Why?" asked Greene, suddenly wary.

"The ritual requires it," said Cope. "Objects which have been in Ayen's presence remain invested with shreds of her power. These are the skulls of the goddess's hounds. The beasts, as you see, are long dead, yet they retain memories of Ayen's former Hound Master. Aspects of Basilis inhabit these memories. To communicate with him we must explore them."

Ravencrag actually yawned.

Cope ignored him. "The ritual is similar to those used by shamans to induce visions. You are familiar with the ways of the Heshette Seers, the bone women of the north?"

"That old coot's familiar with plenty of women from the north," said Ravencrag. "Caused him nothing but trouble."

Nevertheless, Greene acquiesced. What did he have to lose? His life? His eternal soul? Better that than the lives of his family. He pricked his thumb on a needle the thaumaturge produced, then, under Cope's instruction, let a drop fall into the dust inside the hound's skull.

But Ravencrag refused to have anything to do with the ritual.

"You summoned my master here," Cope said to him. "Without your blood, we cannot proceed."

"Shame," said the phantasmacist. "You know where the door is."

Greene felt his anger swell. "You will prick your thumb, or I'll bite off your fucking finger myself. I've not come this far for you to wreck everything!"

The other man grunted.

"You want your bonus?"

Ravencrag did as he was told.

The thaumaturge then scooped the clotted dust into a spoon, and heated it over a candle.

"Shouldn't we be uttering some incantation?" muttered Ravencrag. "Words of power, or some such thing?"

"If you know any incantations," said Cope, "feel free to utter them. I shall not object."

Ravencrag sank deeper into his coat pockets.

The dust smouldered and leaked blue smoke which had an odd, chemical odour. The fumes thickened, becoming a dense cloud around the three men. A candle on the mantel guttered and blew out. Greene laboured to breathe. In the distance he thought he heard the braying of a pack of dogs, the thunder of hooves, and the clatter of steel: the sound of the hunt. Hot, humid air crept over them. They were assailed by powerful odours: of soil, loam, wood and moss.

And then the smoke cleared.

Sal Greene found himself in an oak forest. Sunshine filtered through green leaves, dappling the mossy ground. A breeze rustled the canopy. He spied glimpses of vivid blue sky overhead, yet down here the light was soft and verdant and full of birdsong.

He stumbled and fell onto his rear, gaping at his surroundings. "Is this Heaven?" he exclaimed.

"This place no longer exists," said Cope. "We are inside the dream of the first hound. This was your world, an age ago, when forest covered the Deadsands. Come, quickly now, there are dangers here."

Ravencrag said, "The fucker's drugged us!"

"True," agreed the thaumaturge. "Yet here we are. Curb your tongue. An aspect of Basilis exists beyond these trees. You will show respect, or be cast out."

Greene got to his feet.

Othniel Cope set a jaunty pace. He led the men through the woods, swinging his walking stick at his side. The ground sprung underfoot. Green shadows swayed gently over the forest floor.

After only a short distance, the party came to a clearing in which a huge oak stood on its own. It was much larger and older than the others, yet it looked sick and wasted. Black leaves grew from its gnarled branches. It had queer, blistered bark which glistened and seemed to weep fluids. A fungal infection? The woodland behind it appeared to be similarly afflicted. Disease had crippled the forest, reducing it to a glooming place of mould and shadow.

Greene peered closer at the bole of the oak, then suddenly recoiled. "Those are eyes!" he exclaimed.

The oak was indeed full of eyes. Countless numbers of them peered out from the bark. Several eyes narrowed on the three men; others rolled in their wooden sockets, staring at the heavens and earth. Occasionally one eye, or a dozen, blinked. The prospector suppressed a shiver. He had a hideous impression that he was being studied by something ancient and cunning.

"This sentinel marks the beginning of the Forest of Eyes," said Cope. "The hound remembers its master's gaze. The woodland beyond this point is a representation of that memory, deformed by my master's will where it has subjugated the hound's dream. It is one aspect of the demon, Basilis, which has been preserved." He threw open his arms. "Is it not beautiful?"

Greene chose not to reply.

Beyond the sentinel oak, the woods became very strange indeed. A deathly hush settled around the three men. Greene could no longer hear chirrup of birds or the whisper of leaves. A scrawl of black, twisted trees surrounded him, full of subtle movements. He felt eyes on him constantly, and when he turned to look, there *were* eyes staring at him: eyes in the boles, branches and roots, all moving, turning to follow the party. The demon's forest watched him with furious malevolence.

They walked on a carpet of black mulch, veined with pale fibres. When once Green nudged a scrap of the stuff aside with the toe of his boot, he saw eyes peering out at him from the clammy soil.

"Best not examine the ground too closely," warned Cope. "Lest you fear to tread."

The environment deeply unnerved the old prospector. In his youth, he had travelled to lands beyond Deadsands and had grown skilled at reading the history of the world in its shape and strata. He knew where to look for seams of copper or quartz, and which river banks hid the bones of ancient beasts. He understood erosion, how wind, rain, and ice had sculpted mountain valleys so long ago. But this place was utterly alien to him; it deceived his every sense. He felt tainted by the unwholesomeness of it all. If this was magic, he wanted no part of it.

Ravencrag, however, had evidently forgotten his former antipathy toward Cope. The phantasmacist shuffled through the trees, gazing around in wonder at the wretched place. The staring eyes did not seem to disturb him as much as the pain in his hip. He struggled to keep up, and Cope and Greene were forced to slow their pace to accommodate him, much to the thaumaturge's annoyance. It was this infirmity of Ravencrag's which put them all in danger.

Othniel Cope hissed a warning and flung himself down behind a glutinous tangle of roots. He beckoned the others to join him. Greene did so at once, but Ravencrag, hampered by his stiff joints, was slower. By the time the phantasmacist had hidden himself, it was too late.

A group of very tall figures were approaching through the forest. Greene counted eight of them, all dressed in strange segmented tan-coloured armour, bristling with hairs. Chitinous helmets fitted with dark lenses obscured their faces. None appeared to be armed with martial weapons, yet their hands were protected by wicked spiked gauntlets. The warriors walked in an odd, jerking fashion, as though their legs had too many joints.

"Who are they?" he whispered to Cope.

"I was afraid of this," said the thaumaturge, rising to his feet. "These warriors are an infestation, parasites born from the hound's memories and then mutated here. Such is my master's influence on the hound's dream. Once these creatures were fleas. Come, it is better not to hide. They have already smelled us."

The figures reached them and stood in a semicircle under the watching trees. Greene caught his breath. What he had taken to be armour, was actually exoskeleton. The figures had short forelimbs and powerful legs. Combs twitched in their domed heads where their mouths ought to be.

One of them made a scratching, fluttering noise: "Frrr frnnn, frrr."

Cope strode purposefully towards them, slapping his hands as if to shoo them away. "Leave!" he commanded. "Go! Be gone!"

"Thrrrrrr." The flea-men shifted and twitched; their mouth combs blurred. "Thrrrrr garrrrr."

"They are of low intelligence," explained the thaumaturge. "But dangerous, should they decide to attack as a group. Show no fear or doubt or they will certainly pounce."

"We can be killed?" asked Ravencrag. "By a fucking hallucination?"

"It is a dream, Mr Ravencrag, but it is not our dream. As interlopers, we are bound by the physical laws of this place. Our souls can be damaged here. We can be killed." He clapped his hands at the armoured creatures again, and then raised his walking stick as if to strike one of them. "Get away! Hah! "

"Frrrrrrnn Frrrrrrnn." The creatures flinched, clearly agitated. Most backed away, but one crept closer to the thaumaturge, coiling to pounce.

"Hah!" In a quick, fluid motion, Cope pulled a thin sword from the hollow body of his walking stick and stabbed the thing through its chest. It crumpled to the ground. The thaumaturge put a boot on the body and yanked his blade free. Blood dripped from the steel. Twitching, the other flea-men leapt away. They danced beyond the reach of their attacker's weapon. "Frrrrnnn Thrrrrr Frrrnn Thrrrrr."

"I require assistance, gentlemen," said Cope. "The scent of blood excites them. Stand with me, clap, and shout at them. Show *no* fear! Hah!" He lunged at the nearest creature, forcing it to recoil.

Greene surged forward, slapping his big hands together, and yelling. "Away with you! Away!"

Ravencrag fled.

The phantasmacist, who had previously seemed so infirm, moved with a speed Greene could scarcely believe. His little bowl-shaped hat bobbed as he ran back through the Forest of Eyes, leaving his comrades alone to face their foes.

Clicking and chattering, the flea-men advanced. Cope swung his queer blade, nicking one creature's shoulder, but then the others were on him.

Greene searched wildly around for a weapon. He saw nothing. He saw...

He grabbed at a branch from the nearest tree, and yanked hard. Something popped in his fist, leaking fluid. A rotten stench filled his nostrils, but he ignored it, heaving with all of his might at the branch. The wood cracked and split. He twisted it. Bark peeled away. Another yank and the branch came loose. Greene swung the makeshift club at the nearest attacker, striking it square across its chitinous head. The creature hissed, retreated a step, its glassy eyes fixed on the prospector. Greene raised the club. To his horror, he saw that the branch was glaring at him.

Othniel Cope was having a hard time of it. Six of the creatures had surrounded him. Again and again the thaumaturge struck out with his sword, but the flea-men ducked and wove around his blows. All around him, the Forest of Eyes watched in mute fury, its countless eyes narrowed on the battle.

"Have you no magic to help us?" yelled Greene.

"I don't dare ask Basilis for aid," the thaumaturge cried over his shoulder. He struck out again as one of the creatures swiped at him, driving the foul thing back even as the others pressed closer. "It could be the end of us."

The flea-men chattered and buzzed. "Frrrrnn. Thrrrr."

Greene lashed his club at his own opponent. The wood connected, leaving a wet smear across its segmented face. But it was an impotent weapon against this creature's armour. The prospector could not hope to damage his foe, and already he was tiring. Pain cramped his hands. When had he lost the strength to handle himself in a fight? "It'll be the end of us if you don't do something," he said. "These bastards are relentless."

Cope took down a second attacker with a well-aimed thrust to the neck, but this sent the rest of them into a fury. Two pounced at once, and, while he strove to drive the first one off, the other clung to his side, burrowing its head into his shoulder.

Blood sluiced down the thaumaturge's arm. Impervious to Cope's flailing sword, the creature began to feed.

The thaumaturge cried out. He stumbled backwards, struggling against his attacker. He stabbed at the creature again and again.

Agony wracked Greene's hands. His chest heaved; he could hardly breathe. Yet he rushed to the other man's aid, smashing his club into the flea-man's face.

It would not release its grip.

"Basilis!" cried Cope. "Cast us out!"

The world dimmed. Smoke engulfed Greene, and he felt his awareness leave him. The strength fled from his legs; he crashed to his knees. From the distance came a sound, like the long, low drone of a horn.

O NCE MORE THE OLD prospector found himself in
Ravencrag's suite above the Phantasmacists Club. The
fumes had cleared. It remained dark outside, still warm in here
and lit by the glow of the stove. Othniel Cope and Ravencrag
were slumped in the same chairs where they had been sitting
before, groggy but alive.

Greene felt something heavy in his fist. He was still clutching
the branch from the Forest of Eyes. It looked at him, and at the
ceiling, walls, and floor—all at once. Disgusted, the prospector
let it drop to the floor.

The phantasmacist twitched and groaned.

"Coward!" Greene hissed. "We could have died back there."

Ravencrag rubbed his eyes. "I'm no common brawler," he
snarled. "I'm a fucking scholar, Greene. There's no honour in
scrapping with witless beasts, even in a dream."

"So you took the honourable option of running away?"

Ravencrag spat. "Those fuckers showed no interest in
attacking you until you provoked them."

"You crippled little—"

A sudden cry from Cope interrupted him. The thaumaturge
was hunched over the table. Blood darkened the shoulder of his
topcoat, but he paid his wound no heed. In each hand, he held

a broken piece of the hound's skull. The relic had been cleft in two. Dust trickled between his fingers. "One of Ayen's hounds has been destroyed!" he wailed. "An aspect of my lord, Basilis, is lost. He is diminished!"

Ravencrag fumbled awkwardly with his cuffs. "It's not my fault," he said. "It's not my fucking fault!"

The thaumaturge's eyes thinned. He seemed about to murder the other man, but then something on the floor snagged his attention. "What is this!?" He picked up Greene's branch and glared at it in evident horror.

"I grabbed it to thump those things," said Greene wearily. He could feel every moment of the fight in his old bones. He cricked his neck, then winced and wished he hadn't. "I was still holding the branch when we returned."

"You *ripped* this from the forest?" cried Cope, aghast. "You *assaulted* Ayen's Lord of Warfare? An eternal demon? I…" He shook his head, struggling for words. "In all the decades I have served and obeyed His will, I have never seen such blasphemy, such outrageous contempt!"

"I was only trying to help," said Greene.

"Help?" Cope gagged. Then he snarled, "There will be a heavy price to pay for this, Mr Greene. My master does not look upon such acts of barbarism lightly. You have—" Abruptly he stopped yelling. He knocked back the brim of his hat, and held the grisly piece of wood between both of his hands, examining it closely. When at last he spoke, his voice was soft and full of wonder, "But it is still alive..?"

"Is that good?"

The thaumaturge was muttering excitedly to himself. "Astonishing, quite astonishing," he said. "Do you realise what this means? Basilis found a way to free this aspect of himself from the hound's dream. When you broke a piece from the forest and held it in your hands, he expelled you. But you have returned part of his vision to earth!"

"I am sorry," Greene grumbled.

Cope unbuttoned his topcoat, reached inside, and withdrew the pup from one the garment's many pockets. The dog opened its eyes, blinked, and then cast its gaze around the room. Its unnatural eyes fixed on the prospector. They were furious, the same eyes Greene had seen in the demon's forest.

The pup was an abomination. Greene could not look at it.

"Basilis is no longer blind," the thaumaturge said. "And if my lord can see, then so can I." He set the dog down, and returned his attention to the hideous branch, peering into one of the demon's many eyes.

And then he grinned.

THE MESSAGES CONTINUED to haunt Carnival. She found no escape from them. In every dark attic and abandoned hovel, they cried out to her from the walls.

LIE STRET LYE STR LIE STREET

WHITTEN!

Go to the lye tower.

The moon thinned as the penultimate Scar Night of the year drew near. She could feel the blood quickening in her veins and the hunger reaching up and curling around her heart like ivy. Her time to hunt was close.

Yet the Spine continued to hound her. Armed assassins manned watchtowers in every part of Deepgate. They crawled between the chains and gables of the Warrens. Missiles hissed past her when she took to the skies.

She discovered a chimney stack built above a disused furnace and climbed inside its blackened throat. Twenty feet down she paused, resting awkwardly between two thin protrusions of brick. Her boots dislodged soot, feathers, and silver coins from the ledges, sending them tumbling and clinking into the depths. The chimney stank of burnt coal.

A white envelope had been wedged into a crack in the mortar. She teased it loose then stared at it for long time, her apprehension growing. Something made her open it and read the note inside. Beneath a sketch of a knife, she read:

Look in your pockets.

There was nothing in her pockets! Nothing! She tore the paper to shreds and fled the chimney.

And so she resolved to avoid the decaying and abandoned places of Deepgate. She flew to the sand-blown streets of the labourers' encampment on the edge of the abyss.

The settlement had been constructed above the very lip of the chasm, where the great sapperbane chain anchors had been driven deep into the bedrock. Heaps of rock, timber, and lime glowed by the light of braziers, throwing massive shadows over the wasteland beyond. Cloth tents stood in amber ranks, the flaps sewn shut. A few men huddled in groups, drinking and smoking, but Carnival crept away from them, out to the fringes where the firelight couldn't reach her.

She ducked under Deepgate's main water pipe and stood at the perimeter of everything mankind had made, gazing out across the Deadsands. Dunes stretched to the horizon, bone-coloured under the waning moon. Here and there, the branches of petrified trees reached up from the sand to clutch at the heavens. Nothing but the stars lay beyond.

The vast emptiness of the wasteland filled her with a new fear. How could there be so many leagues of *nothing*? Her anguish engulfed her, became a sudden desperate panic. She

gasped and clawed at her chest, fighting the urge
to return to the city.

"Hello."

Carnival wheeled.

A little girl stood there, one hand
resting nervously against the base of the
water pipe. She was five or six years old,
barefoot and dressed in the same brown rags
the camp labourers wore. She wore flowers in
her tangled hair. Her eyes were wide; she had half-
turned away, as if to be ready to flee. She gaped at Carnival's
wings, then at the scars on her face. "You're the bad angel,"
she said.

Carnival stared.

A call came from somewhere close by, "Noona!"

The girl glanced away, then back at Carnival. "What's wrong
with your face?"

"Noona!"

A woman ducked under the pipe. She was slim with long
brown hair, barefooted like the girl. "Noona, there you are," she said
crossly. "How many times have I told you—" She saw the angel.

Carnival did not move.

The woman grabbed the child, scooping her roughly up in
her arms. "Stay away from her! Stay the fuck away from her!"

The girl began to cry.

The woman stumbled backwards in the sand, her back
grazing the water pipe. "You stay the fuck away from my
daughter, you ugly bitch!"

Carnival took a step back. A desert breeze stirred her feathers.

"Mommy…" the girl sobbed.

"Leave us alone!" the woman screamed.

The angel leapt into the night sky, thrashing her wings. Beneath her she saw men running, firebrands moving between the rows of tents. She heard shouts and curses, the screaming mother, and the child's wails. "Mommy!" She flew higher, higher, dragging herself up beyond the range of arrows, and out over the dark, rusting bowl of the city.

Deepgate waited in its chains, a thousand blinking lights around the towering mass of the temple. The angel tore through the sky, out over the League of Rope and the Workers' Warrens. Chains ticked and groaned beneath her. Shadows waited in every lane and behind every link and girder; they seemed to reach for her. Carnival flew on, her chest numb, her scarred flesh cold and bloodless. She could not think of a single place to go.

RAVENCRAG REFUSED to accommodate the thaumaturge. "It was your fucking idea to bring him here," he whispered to Greene while they stood by the hearth, casting nervous glances back at their unusual guest. Othniel Cope had not moved in an hour. He was squatting on the floor, gazing feverishly at unimaginable sights through his horrible branch. "Besides," Ravencrag added, "you've got a spare room."

Was this punishment, Greene wondered, for his assault on Ravencrag's twisted sense of honour? Or had the phantasmacist begun to fear their guest? The trip to the Forest of Eyes had sickened the prospector, but this new development worried him. He'd inadvertently recovered part of a creature which had no business being loose in this world, a demon who had betrayed both Ayen and Ulcis. And neither of the gods would be very happy about that.

"I have a family," said Greene. "I don't want that creepy bastard near them."

Ravencrag snorted. "And I don't want him near *me*," he hissed. "You should have thought about all this before you brought me the fucking grimoire. Look at him, sitting there with his goddamn branch…The goddamn fucking branch *you* brought back."

Cope was gazing, slack-eyed, into the branch. His skin had an unhealthy waxy sheen to it. He seemed not to breathe.

"What do you reckon he can see?" asked Greene. "Is he watching this world, or another?"

"How the fuck should I know?"

They tried to bring Othniel Cope out if his catatonic state. They could not prise his fingers away from the branch, or his eyes from those of the demon, but he rose to his feet when guided, and walked in any direction in which they steered him.

"He seems docile enough," observed Ravencrag. "Maybe we should just kill him and pitch him into the abyss. I know just the—"

"It's a week till Scar Night," Greene reminded him. "I need the bastard alive."

"Then get him out of here. This is your problem, Sal. If you don't get him the fuck out of my house, I'll call the city militia."

No amount of protest would change Ravencrag's mind. There was nothing for it but to take the thaumaturge back to Greene's house in Lye Street while the neighbourheed was still quiet. He would put Cope in the spare room—or a closet, or one of the large trunks he kept in the attic—lock him in, and wait till he decided to come out of his trance.

They reached Greene's home without incident. The prospector trudged up the steps to his front door just as the sun swelled over the abyss rim, bathing the falcons on the summit of Barraby's watchtower in golden light. At the southern end of the street, the old brick lye tower remained shrouded in gloom. Laundry lines zigzagged between the tenements, all empty and wet with dew. Othniel Cope did not resist as the prospector guided him inside and clicked the door shut behind him.

Jack was already up. His voice called out from the kitchen. "A good night, Sal?"

"Morning, Jack."

"You want some porridge? It's warm."

"No thanks." Greene steered the thaumaturge to the kitchen door. "Jack...this is Othniel Cope, a friend of mine. He'll be staying with us for a while."

Jack looked up from his breakfast. He was a lanky young man, all elbows, with curly dark hair and an open, cheerful face which clouded a little at the sight of their guest. "Good to meet you, Sir." Then he noticed Cope's catatonia and the blank fixation he had with the branch in his hands. Jack's brow creased; he glanced nervously at Greene.

"The man's a thaumaturge," said Greene. "Don't even ask me about the branch. It's a religious thing. Help me get him upstairs before Ellie wakes up."

They sat Cope on a rug by the hearth in Greene's own bedroom, where the prospector reckoned he could keep an eye on him. Jack said nothing about the branch, but he was clearly agitated when he left for work. The heathens had been known to worship all manner of queer objects.

Exhausted, Greene collapsed on his bed and promptly fell asleep in his clothes.

H E WOKE TO FIND amber sunlight slanting through
this window. He had slept until late afternoon. A pitcher
of fresh water and a glass had been left on the table beside his
bed. His heavy topcoat had been removed and placed on a chair
beside the hearth. Cope was nowhere to be seen.

The prospector leapt to his feet.

Ellie was busy in the day room, darning one of Mina's socks.
She glanced up and smiled as he entered. "Mr Cope has been
entertaining us with tales of Dalamoor," she said with a nod to
the thaumaturge, who was seated opposite her, sipping a cup
of tea. A tray of sandwiches and sweetmeats lay on the table
between them. "It sounds so exotic!" she added.

Cope gave the prospector a congenial nod. "I hope you don't
mind," he said. "I didn't want to disturb you, and your daughter
was kind enough to offer me lunch. I was just explaining how
you knew my father and had offered to help find me work in
Deepgate."

Greene wondered what the thaumaturge had done with his
branch. "Where's Mina?" he asked, but then he heard a giggle
and turned to see his granddaughter playing happily in the
corner of the room. Mina was bouncing the thaumaturge's pup
on her lap. She'd dressed up the horrid little thing. The demon

Basilis, Ayen's Lord of Warfare and Hound Master of Heaven, glared out from the frills of one of Mina's doll's frocks. Pink ribbons and bangles decorated its ragged ears.

"Granda!" Mina cried, holding up the puppy in her dumpy little arms. "Dis is Mr Bangles!"

The pup growled.

"Cuddle time," Mina squealed. She hugged the dog against her chest, half strangling it.

"Mina, sweetheart…" Greene began.

"She's perfectly safe," Cope said matter-of-factly. "Basilis has no teeth or claws." The corners of his lips curled in a dangerous smile. "At least, not yet."

T
HAT NIGHT SEVERAL FAMILIES in the Callow district of the city heard screams issuing from an old pendulum house, long abandoned since two of its support chains had snapped and dragged the lower stories into the abyss nine years before. They had checked their own door locks and the bolts on their window shutters, and, on the morrow, when the sun had been high enough to make them feel secure, the men had ventured out to investigate. Blood was seen dripping from the base of the building. A group of concerned citizens marched out to the Church of Ulcis to demand an audience with Presbyter Scrimlock.

Bartholomew Scrimlock listened politely to their concerns, and then dispatched a group of his priests to clean up the blood and locate the victim's family. He reassured the citizens: as Scar Night was still five days away, it was highly unlikely that Carnival was the murderer; it was probably just the work of a common cutthroat. The citizens grumbled, but left.

But Scrimlock was left wondering. It seemed to him that their renegade angel had become even crueller and more vicious of late. Only recently he'd had reports that Carnival had attacked a mother and her child by the water pipe in the abyss rim labourers' camp. Had she started to kill on other nights of the month?

Now he stood before the window in his library, watching the sun set over Deepgate's grey gables, over the watchtowers his predecessor had commissioned, and he wondered briefly whether he ought to risk the life of another temple battle archon.

No. Hadn't Carnival cut through enough of them already?

Scrimlock's cassock sat heavy on his shoulders. All these troubles were aging him prematurely. He had lost the vigour from his step, the humour from his voice. His thick brown hair was peppered with grey; it made him look older than his thirty eight years. His hands had developed a nervous twitch; he rubbed at spots behind his knuckles which were not there, and he worried too much about Hell.

Too much blood had been spilled in Deepgate. Parts of the city were now rife with apparitions. Phantasms haunted murder scenes like the echoes of screams. A gentlemen's club had sprung up in Ivygarths to study these ghosts. Scrimlock took their reports, their analyses and suggestions, and he locked them in his Codex pillars with all the other books submitted for Church appraisal. He never read them with the same gusto he devoured the scientific tomes, for the metaphysical did not interest him as much as the physical: the nuts and bolts of industry which had built his marvellous city.

A sad smile came to his lips. The Spine, if they knew his penchant for engineering, might have him deposed. After all, wasn't he was supposed to be a priest?

Yet hadn't his workers performed miracles? Deepgate's chains were the greatest monument to Church power. They would last for millennia, holding the faithful suspended above their god, until Ulcis was ready to lead them through the gates of Heaven and claim his throne. If man's indomitable determination could create such a city, could it not find a way to kill one scarred little angel?

There was a knock at the door. Adjunct Merryweather entered. A grim expression on his face, the priest glided towards his master, the hem of his deep red cassock dragging across the stones.

"Success?" asked Scrimlock.

"Just another cutthroat job," he said. "The locals are now saying it was a righteous assassination, a response to the murder of the ox carriage driver who plummeted from the rim."

"And was justice served? Did the right person die?"

"Does it matter? The commoners are satisfied."

"Excellent. I like things to be tidy. Is there enough blood left for a Sending?"

"I'm afraid not."

The Presbyter's hands twitched. *More ghosts.*

He sat down at his desk and opened the *Book of Unaccounted Souls*, the tome he called *Carnival's Book* since she had been responsible for almost all of the names in it. "I had wondered if our angel was responsible for this one," he remarked. "She has been taking a lot of Warreners recently."

"It's all the new construction work," said Merryweather. "People are living in unfinished homes. How can they expect to keep her out when they don't yet have a roof over their heads?"

"There are the temple boltholes…"

"They cost a halfpenny a night," replied the Adjunct. "People are reluctant to pay. They prefer to hide and hope for the best."

"A dangerous lottery."

Merryweather withdrew a scroll from his sleeve and handed it to the Presbyter. "The cutthroat's victim."

"Such a waste." Scrimlock began to copy the victim's details into the book. *Sophie Mean, twenty years old, ox carriage driver.* "She was probably a rival of the chap who fell," he muttered.

"What an unfortunate name she had." He added the location of her demise, scribbled the date beside it, and then drew a small cross to indicate Carnival's innocence. It was the only cross on the page. "Perhaps we should abolish the bolthole charges," he muttered. "At least in the poorer districts."

"If we don't charge, we'll have to increase taxes again," explained the Adjunct, "or leave the Warrens incomplete." He shrugged. "And if the boltholes were free, we'd have more people clamouring at their doors than we can safely accommodate. As it is, the lower orders are left to fend for themselves."

"You mean the tinkers and scroungers?"

"Precisely."

The Presbyter stopped writing. "Why doesn't she kill more of *them*? I mean, we've more of these people than is strictly sanitary. They're flinging up shacks and hovels whenever we turn our back, faster than we can drag the wretched things down."

"They smear themselves with glue," replied Merryweather. "Some of them even drink the stuff, claiming it keeps them safe. They say she's no taste for glue-blood." He shrugged again. "That may be true, but the glue kills as many as it saves."

"And do we tax glue?"

"Of course," said Merryweather. "But they buy it from heathen shamans and smuggle it in."

Scrimlock shook his head. There had to be a better way to keep his taxpayers safe. If the tinkers and scroungers wanted to poison themselves with glue, that was fine by him; after all, this League of Rope which had sprung up around the city centre was becoming a fire hazard. But the taxpayers paid for the rock, iron, and mortar which built the city. They ought to be protected.

He dismissed Merryweather and leafed through the pages before him. The records stretched back centuries: hundreds and thousands of names, the men, women and children whose souls would never find their way to Heaven. Such a terrible waste of life. He traced a finger down one page, reading the locations: a butcher's store in Fleshmarket, an attic in Pickle Lane, Samuel's watchtower. He hunted through the older records: Plum Street, Candlemaker Street, Givengair Bridge, Callow. Carnival always chose a different location to bleed her victims. As Deepgate had grown, so had the area in which the corpses had been discovered. Not once had the angel returned to the scene of a murder.

Was she *avoiding* these locations? If so, how did she *remember* to avoid them? Carnival suffered from amnesia. She could not remember traps, a failing the Spine continually used to their advantage.

He could not see how such a discovery might help him, so Scrimlock searched through the victim's names: Yellowfeather, Stone, Tannay, Leatherman, Wellman, Onetree, Portish. He discerned no pattern. The dead appeared to come from all walks of life, from the noblest families to those who were quite clearly the descendants of heathens. There appeared to be some repetitions of the most common names, but that was to be expected.

Next he perused the victim's addresses, all streets Scrimlock knew well from his years on the census board. He flipped back-wards through the pages of the ledger, idly recalling images of the places in his mind, imagining the people who had lived there for generations: Roundhorn from Lilley, Cripp of Morning Road.

He paused.

Morning Road? The name struck a chord. Hadn't there been a great fire there hundreds of years ago, some problem with a cultist or lunatic who thought he'd been pursued by demons? He thumbed back a few pages, then some more, and then finally stopped at the entry he was looking for. A Henry Bucklestrappe

from Morning Road had been
killed in 512. Wasn't that
the very madman who'd
started the fire?

Both street
and surname
name appeared
again several
pages later. The victim
this time was a
Norman Bucklestrappe;
the date, 562. Could
it be coincidence
that two people
sharing the same
address and surname
had been murdered fifty
years apart?

Fifty years?

He returned to the
entry which had originally
grabbed his attention.
Nellie Cripp of Morning
Road had been killed in 612, exactly fifty years after Norman
Bucklestrappe, one hundred years after Henry. Carnival had
returned three times to the same street.

Quickly, he turned to the records for 662.

His heart sank. In all twelve Scar Night entries, there
was no mention of a victim from Morning Road. But then he
noticed a Jack Cripp of Silver Street in Callow. Could he be
Nellie's son? Was Carnival persecuting a *family* rather than a

place, returning every fifty years to kill another descendant? Had Nellie's surname changed from Bucklestrappe to Cripp when she married?

But how did Carnival *know* that?

Frantically, the Presbyter searched forward another fifty years.

John Cripp of Silver Street, died in 712. Anne Wrightman of Silver Street in 762. Another victim followed; then a third, and a fourth, each one killed fifty years after their ancestor. By matching either the victim's name or address, Scrimlock could trace the sequence of murders like links in a chain. As he turned to the final page in the journal, a sudden fear gripped him.

It was 1012 now.

But most of the year had already gone. If Carnival had already killed her victim, they would have to wait another five decades for her to strike again.

Fifty years ago, the victim had been Mack Greene of Lye Street, descended on his mother's side from the Wrightmans, and therefore an ancestor of Henry Bucklestrappe himself. Scrimlock scanned the records for 1012 and reached his own last entry with a sigh of relief. Neither the surname nor the address appeared on this year's listing. Did Mack Greene's family still live in Lye Street?

He rang the bell chord to summon Merryweather back. They had only a few days until the next Scar Night, but that ought to be enough time to find the descendant of a madman and, possibly, save his life.

R AVENCRAG THREW UP HIS arms. "No fucking way!"
Cope and Greene had thumped on the phantasmacist's
door for a good ten minutes before he'd admitted them. In the
end, it had been Cope who'd persuaded the phantasmacist to
open up. He'd done this with not so subtle threats.

The thaumaturge said, "I cannot retrieve Basilis without
you help, Mr Ravencrag. A drop of your blood began the ritual,
and so I require further drops from both of you gentlemen to
proceed. We have escaped the Forest of Eyes, yet there are still
the memories of two hounds to explore."

"And there's your bonus to consider," Greene added.

"Fuck the bonus," said Ravencrag. "I'm staying here."

"You forget," said Cope, "that my lord Basilis has seen you.
He knows you were instrumental in releasing his vision from
the dream of the first hound, albeit in a limited sense. He may
even be grateful. Yet two aspects of the demon remain trapped,
in the Forest of Teeth and the Forest of War. Would you have
me explain to my master how you refused to proceed, how you
abandoned him in his hour of need?"

"He has us there," said Greene.

Ravencrag stabbed a finger at him. "No. He has *you* there.
You want to go back! There's only two Scar Nights left in the

year and that fucking angel is going to come for your blood on one of them. *You've* got nothing to lose." He shook his head. "Sorry, Sal, but you're on your own. I won't do it."

"So be it," said Cope. "I wish you a long and happy life, Mr Ravencrag. Although, since you have chosen to make an enemy of my master, I doubt you'll have either."

"Wait a minute," Ravencrag said quickly. "You said that without both Sal's blood and mine you can't finish the ritual. Right? We can't release Basilis?"

"Correct."

The phantasmacist looked relieved. "Then having him as an enemy doesn't mean shit. What's the mutt going to do? Glare at me?"

"Mr Ravencrag, I don't think you understand. I intend to use your blood with or without your permission. My master would have looked more kindly upon you if the blood had been offered willingly." Cope unsheathed his gut-sticker.

"Hey! Just a—"

Cope jabbed the tip of the blade into Ravencrag's shoulder "Ow!"

Cope brandished the weapon's bloody tip. "Thank you, Mr Ravencrag," he said. "Mr Greene and I will return when we need some more."

The phantasmacist grumbled and rubbed his shoulder. "Damn you, Cope, that hurt." He chewed his lips. "If I help you to release him…willingly, I mean. What'll happen to me?"

"Basilis may decide to reward you," replied Cope, "or he may punish you for all eternity."

Judging by the Ravencrag's expression, this was not the response he had hoped for. "And if I don't help to release him?"

"Certain punishment."

The phantasmacist thought for a long moment. Then he faced Greene. "You and your fucking grimoire." he said.

A FIERCE NORTHERN WIND dragged clouds across the heavens, obscuring stars and moon. Deepgate's chains whistled. In places streets and houses rocked gently in their ironwork cradles, while out in the League, the ropes and walkways flapped and creaked. The end of autumn often brought such winds from the north, carrying rain across the Deadsands and the promise of colder weather to come.

Carnival heard music.

An eerie melody floated across the chained city. Mournful yet discordant, the song seemed to rise and fall with the wind.

The angel had never heard anything so beautiful before. Curious, she flew towards the sound.

The district of Bridgeview encircled the Church of Ulcis. Whitewashed townhouses overlooked that moat of air and chains around the temple itself. Space here was limited, and the buildings had scrambled over each other's shoulders to fill it. Gables elbowed chimney stacks. Walls shouldered walls, nudging stone work this way and that. Windows glared at each other in mute defiance. Even the tangle of chains stitching it all together looked like the result of a war among weavers. It was an ongoing contest among the noble families who lived there, a slow but steady conflict waged over hundreds of years.

Normally Carnival would not have flown so close to the temple. Spine assassins used the naked foundation chains to travel to and fro that monstrous building. Yet the mournful music intrigued her. Swallowing her fears, she flew on, and soon discovered the source of the lament.

A terrace near the summit of a ramshackle dwelling had been filled with crystal wine flutes of various sizes, the vessels placed side by side so as to cover every inch of the paving stones. Gusts of wind plucked notes from this strange arrangement of glass and carried them across the city. Was this intended to be a warning system against club-footed intruders? Such a measure seemed excessive given the proximity of the temple. Carnival crouched on the terrace balustrade and looked up at the vast dark building, at its gargoyles and blazing windows. Scaffolding clung to the stonework, rising to reckless heights.

Each flute had been polished to high sheen. Light spilling under the roof terrace door illuminated crystal stems. Someone was inside the house. The angel almost fled back to the derelict places she had come to fear. But she stopped. Above the door, half obscured by ivy, an open hatch led to what appeared to be a storage space under the roof.

She padded along the balustrade and peered into the hole.

It was hardly an attic, more of a triangular tunnel, but it was invitingly gloomy. Carnival's uncanny vision probed the depths of it, but she couldn't see any messages.

She folded her wings against her back and climbed inside.

Silently, so as not to disturb the occupants in the rooms below, she crawled along the tunnel on her hands and knees. Through cracks in the floorboards she caught glimpses of a hallway leading back into the house.

The tunnel opened into a larger chamber, shaped like the

inside of a pyramid. Apart from a water tank in one corner, the space was stuffed with thousands of rings. There were huge mounds of them, all gleaming gold and silver. Some boasted cut gemstones and elaborate filigree, while others were just plain.

Carnival picked one up and examined it. It was old and tarnished. On the inside it bore an engraving:

To E.B, with love.

She frowned, and replaced the ring on one of the piles.

Why would anyone hoard such trinkets?

And why leave the roof hatch open?

A creak from the room below grabbed her attention. Carnival froze. She listened for a long time, but heard no other sounds. The floor here was old and warped, allowing her to peer down through one of the gaps.

An opulent study lay below the attic, lit by brass gasoliers and a fire in a black stone hearth. Dyed catskin rugs covered the floorboards. Turning her head, the angel spied a bookcase, some shelves, and a display cabinet packed with brightly-coloured stuffed birds: yellow and green mottled songbirds, red tops, canaries, and the like. A second, larger, glass-fronted case rested against the opposite wall, this also full of exotic specimens. Between the cabinets, an elderly lady sat at a desk before the window drapes. She was facing away from Carnival, peering through a lens at something on her desk. Then she set the lens down, and cocked her head to one side, listening.

"Back again?" the old lady said. "I wondered when you'd return."

Carnival held her breath.

"There's no need to skulk up there in the attic." Her grey hair had been tied up in a bunch and she wore a black frock with white frills at the cuffs and neck, yet Carnival could not see her face.

The old lady went on, "I won't harm you, dear. Why don't you go back the way you came and enter through the door? I'll dim the lights so they don't hurt your eyes, then we can chat like civilised people."

Carnival didn't know what to do. Her instincts told her to flee, but another darker part of her heart screamed a warning: *A trick! A trap! Silence the crone, now, before her cries alert the Spine.* This house lay too close to the temple. The attic floor would be easy enough to rip through. She could tear out the woman's neck and...

And what?

Where would Carnival go?

The crone rose from her seat. "Come now, go out and walk back in through the door like a sensible girl," she said in clipped, authoritative tones. "I'll make us a nice pot of tea."

Carnival hesitated.

A long moment passed. Finally the old lady said, "The rings are from the dead. Marriage rings. The priests retrieve them for me before casting the corpses into the abyss. They do this because I ask them to."

"Why?" The angel's voice sounded hoarse, strange to her own ears. She could not remember the last time she'd used it.

The old lady grunted. "Why do I ask them? Or why do they pander to my requests?"

Carnival said nothing.

"I ask them," the lady said, "because there is power in such objects. I believe we should keep a little of our dead back from God: just a trinket, some intimate little thing the soul has brushed on its way through life. By doing so we maintain a link with Him, so we can understand and love Him more. The priests bring me the rings because they have no conception of their true value. And because I provide a valuable service for them."

"What?"

The old lady sighed. "Your memory frustrates me," she said softly. "You should know me by now, dear. We have had this conversation many, many times before." Then she turned and looked directly up at the angel. She was a striking woman with a slender jaw and high cheek bones. Her gaze met Carnival's squarely, with no hint of fear or revulsion in her violet eyes.

Carnival thought there was something familiar about her.

The old lady smiled kindly. "Come down and talk with me, child. Some call me a witch, but you have no reason to fear or distrust me. My name is Ruby, and I knew your mother a long time ago."

Her mother?

"A thousand years ago," said Ruby. "Back when Deepgate's chains were forged, I made a promise to her to look out for you; to keep you safe if I could. I can help you, dear. I can make all that is ugly about you beautiful."

Carnival remained wary. She had no memory of her childhood or parents, even in her dreams. When she slept she dreamt of chains and knives and blood. More likely the witch meant Carnival harm. Everyone meant the angel harm. Yet what if this old woman was speaking the truth? What was it about her face Carnival found so familiar?

I can help you, dear.

"I know you have been plagued by messages lately." Ruby's violet eyes twinkled. "They make demands of you, don't they? And you suspect you know who the author is, eh? Yet you're too afraid to accept the truth. Maybe I can help to make the messages go away."

Outside, the crystal glasses trembled and chimed. Carnival retraced her steps through the attic and came back into the house through the roof terrace door, as she had been asked to do.

The witch's study was snug and smelled of lavender. Her display cabinets faced each other across the floor, the stuffed songbirds positioned on branches and twigs, all peering out with glittering glass eyes.

Ruby hung a kettle on a hook over the hearth, and then turned to face Carnival. "Oh my," she said. "Oh you poor child! I had forgotten how many Scar Nights have passed since we last met, but I see every one of them now in the cuts on your face." She lifted a hand to touch Carnival's cheek.

Carnival recoiled.

The witch lowered her hand. "You mustn't be afraid. What harm can a frail old thing like me cause *you,* the strongest of all angels?" Slowly, she brought her hand up again. This time Carnival did not flinch away.

"So many scars," murmured Ruby, running her fingers gently across the lesions on Carnival's cheek. "So many lives taken." She cupped the angel's chin softly in her hand. "This is a mask, child," she said softly, and then with vigour: "And if you can wear one mask, then surely you can wear another?" She released Carnival. "Let's forego the tea for now. We have a great deal of work to do, so I suggest we begin at once."

Carnival's skin tingled. She had never allowed another person to touch her before.

The witch became full of energy and determination. "We can cover the scars and lift that horrid pallor from your skin with make-up and rouge. Your hair? Hah! It's like a crow's nest! A wash and comb will soon fix that. Your eyes are quite pretty, in a dark, brooding sort of way. They just need a spot of colour around them. I have just what we need in my dresser."

She beckoned Carnival into the next room.

But the angel was looking at the desk where the witch had been sitting. A small bird had been fixed to its surface, the wings stretched out and secured to the wood with silver pins. One wing was dull and grey, but the other was quite beautiful, with brilliant hues of yellow and red. Then Carnival noticed the jars of colourful paint on a shelf beside the desk, and a pot full of tiny brushes, and she understood what had happened.

"A little hobby of mine," said the witch.

Carnival followed the old lady. At the door she glanced back one last time at the little painted bird, with its tiny dead eyes.

WHEN THE SMOKE CLEARED, Greene found himself surrounded by woodland once more. Autumn, or what passed for seasons in this place, had turned the trees to shades of gold and copper. The sky was a very pale yellow, and sunlight fell through the canopy in amber spears. The smell of old leaves and earth hung heavy in the air.

"The Forest of Teeth?" he asked.

"Think of this as an antechamber," said Cope. "Here the hound's memories are strongest, but as we proceed, you will see that Basilis's influence consumes the beast's dream. The demon's aspect is quite beautiful here."

"You reckon teeth are beautiful?" Ravencrag spat on the ground. "Maybe to a hag who lacks her own...."

"Ignore him," said Green. "He misses his courting days."

The thaumaturge laughed.

"Are we likely to encounter more of those flea-men?" asked Greene.

"Doubtful," said Cope. "They fear the Forest of Teeth, and the things which dwell there."

"Well my mind's at rest," said Greene. "Let's get it over with."

They marched over a carpet of crisp dry leaves. Ahead through the trees there appeared to be another clearing. Greene saw flashes of light there, shapes glittering like silver, or mirrors. He thought he heard a sound in the air, like faint music.

Cope stopped and scratched the brim of his tall hat.

"What is it?" asked Greene.

"I've just had worrying thought"

"About something that lies ahead?"

Cope nodded. "We didn't bring tools." He set off again.

The prospector exchanged a glance with the phantasmacist, then followed the other man into the clearing.

It was a tree of swords. This sentinel stood in the centre of a circle of dry earth, its steel branches glittering under the pale sky. The lower part of the trunk had been wrapped in stained leather cord, like the grip of a heavily used weapon. Long thin blades jutted from it at every angle, which in turn sprouted smaller and smaller blades, like knives and needles. By the size and curve of each branch, Greene took them to be bastard swords, cutlasses, daggers and stilettos, all beautifully forged and polished to a mirror-like sheen.

Beyond the tree lay a wicked forest of metal, a thicket so dazzling as to be painful to look upon. The trees crowded together in the sunshine, a vast hedge of razor sharp edges. Greene couldn't see a way through it.

"My master was fond of his weapons," said Cope. "As you see, the hound remembers, although this representation has been altered by Basilis. These are the teeth of the demon. We must be wary. My master may protect us from the forest. Then again, he might choose to sacrifice either of you. It's often hard to tell."

Ravencrag growled in his throat. "I'm not fucking walking through that."

"Then please remain here," said Cope. "Should you encounter Wirralwights, Red Spleeners or Needlechildren, or even—Gods forbid—Armstrong Hackwish and his three blind wives, I trust you will remember to make the appropriate signs before you flee? These creatures are not as witless as fleas."

"I rue the day I met you, Cope."

The three men walked into the forest of swords, following the thaumaturge, who led them along a narrow track through the steel. A cold breeze blew, shivering the metal. The trees rasped. Needles tinkled. Everything glittered and flashed, making Greene feel dizzy and disoriented. He saw reflections in the blades all around: of his own haggard face, Ravencrag's scowl, and Cope's sardonic smile. He smelled steel, and the sweat from the leather-bound boles. Sharp edges crowded in on them, threatening to slice their shoulders. Even the ground over which they travelled felt hard and jagged underfoot. In places, the tips of swords broke through the cracked earth and split the soles of Greene's boots. The prospector wrapped his heavy topcoat around himself. He decided he would rather not be forced to flee through this cruel forest.

"Why don't we just grab one of these branches?" he said to Othniel Cope.

"By all means, try," replied Cope.

The prospector eyed a likely tree: a monstrous, buckled thing bristling with serrated long swords, short swords, rapiers, foils, and a brilliant canopy of knives and tiny daggers.

He pressed the heels of both hands against the flat of a good-sized blade, and pushed. The metal flexed, but remained firmly fixed to the tree. He reached around the steel to pull it towards him, and winced in sudden pain. A line of blood welled across his left palm. He cursed and squeezed the hand under his armpit. "Razor sharp," he said.

"I could have told you that," muttered Ravencrag.

"Well thanks for the warning."

The thaumaturge tipped his hat further back on his head. "As I thought," he said. "My master wishes us to take a particular sword; one which best encompasses the aspect of himself represented by this forest. It will be a blade of superb quality, I imagine, and not a common gut-sticker."

"He didn't require us to take a particular branch from the last place," said Greene. "I just ripped off the first bit of wood which came to hand."

"At the time," said Cope, "Basilis was unaware that his vision could be removed from the hounds' dream. Who could have predicted that your vandalism would free a part of him? I would never have assaulted one of my master's trees.

"If Basilis had foreseen the consequences of your actions, I think he would have preferred you to choose a more suitable branch, one with many more eyes, perhaps, or clearer vision."

"So which sword does he want us to take?"

Cope thought for a moment. "I shall ask him to guide us."

He opened his topcoat, removed the branch, and peered into it. After a long moment he exclaimed, "This way, gentlemen!"

And so the demonic branch led them through the forest of steel. The land sloped down into a shallow basin or valley. Overhead the sky changed from yellow to a peculiar fragile pink, a hue reflected in the polished trees. All turned pink: the metal boughs, the gleaming roots, the cruel points pushing up through the earth. As they descended the air became bitterly cold. A smell of oil or some other such preservative infused the forest. The further they went, the more the breeze strengthened, until a freezing wind was howling through the woodland, causing branches to shiver and clash.

Ravencrag held on to his hat. "This is madness."

"The gale is my master's lust for violence," shouted Cope. "Invigorating, is it not?"

"Fucking cold is what it is," cried Ravencrag. "I can't feel my hands. Sal, how about lending me your coat?"

"Get lost, Laccus."

They came upon pool of clear water, its surface rippling with the force of the gale. It appeared to be no more than a few inches deep, yet stretched far into the trees ahead, turning the forest into swamp. In places, clumps of knives and silver spears sprouted from the water, like metal grasses and reeds. Greene stooped to wash his lacerated hand, but the thaumaturge grabbed his shoulder. "You have an open wound," explained Cope, "and nothing in this place is what it seems."

But just as the prospector rose, something curious caught his attention. A small island, no more than a mound of bleached earth, broke the surface of the waters. The hummock was bare, but for a single short sword which sprouted from its apex, the tip pointing at the sky. The weapon looked modest, with a plain pommel and a simple cross-shaped guard, yet the blade shone like a beacon.

Cope had followed the prospector's gaze. "In a forest of giants, we find a sapling."

"You reckon this is the sword we're supposed to take?"

"I am sure of it, Mr Greene."

Ravencrag hawked up a gob of phlegm, swilled it round his mouth, then spat into the blowing water. "The demon leads us all the way here and he doesn't put some flea-men, or clickety sword beasts, or some other evil bastard in our path? We just take the sword and go?"

"Why not?" said Cope.

"I don't like it," muttered Ravencrag. "The whole thing stinks."

"You sound disappointed," said Greene.

The phantasmacist did not reply. He yanked his little black hat further down over his eyes, then stuffed his hands deep into his coat pockets.

Cope waded into the pool. After a moment's hesitation, the old prospector followed. He gave an involuntary gasp as freezing water seeped into his boots, yet the ground remained solid underfoot. The sound of splashing water accompanied the whistling gale and clashing branches. He glanced back at Ravencrag. "You're not coming?"

"With my bones?" the phantasmacist yelled. "Certainly not! And I'll thank you not to call me a coward just because I don't want to get my feet wet. I hope you catch your fucking death." He eased himself down onto the hard ground, but then leapt suddenly to his feet. "Gods in Hell!" he cried. "The ground has fucking knives in it. That went right up my arse!"

Greene grinned. He reached the island moments after Cope and squatted beside him. The sword was unadorned, as modest as it had looked from the shore, with a plain, functional hilt and guard, and a clean, sharp blade. Yet there is beauty in simplicity. This sword had been forged—or grown—for combat rather than show. The edge and tip of the blade looked as keen as any the prospector had seen. It would be easy to push such steel into a man.

Cope grabbed the weapon's hilt and gave it a tug. The sword did not move.

"How do we get it out?" asked Greene.

"Hmm." Gingerly, the thaumaturge brushed earth away from the base of the pommel. "There appears to be a root system," he said.

"Can we dig round it?"

Cope continued to expose more steel from the surrounding ground. The pommel was not as simple as it had first appeared: it was connected to a complex arrangement of metal shoots beneath the earth.

"The roots have no function," Cope observed, squatting back on his haunches. "Yet our hound knows that trees have roots, and so this sword has been given roots in its dream. We only *need* to return with the sword, so we must find a way to separate it from the earth without causing damage." His brow creased with concern. "I should have considered this problem more carefully before we arrived."

"Let me try." The prospector gave the weapon's grip a mighty kick with the heel of his boot. A hideous metal peal rang out across the swamp. The steel bent, below the pommel, but the sword, although now skewed, remained attached to the ground.

Cope gasped. "You have just assaulted Ayen's Lord of Warfare a second time!" he cried. "Is no amount of brutish vandalism against my master beyond you?"

"Worked in the Forest of Eyes," said Greene, who had always been of the opinion that if something valuable was stuck in the ground, a crack with a pickaxe was the best way of getting the damn thing out.

"Yes, I am sure the demon Basilis has not forgotten the way you ripped out his eyes to batter a flea in the face. Just as I am convinced that the kick you have now administered to his teeth will reverberate in his memory for some time to come."

Now Greene understood why Cope's pup had glared at him with such profound malevolence. Notwithstanding the fact that he'd *helped* the demon, the thing was pissed at him for hurting it. Basilis's impending release from captivity had just acquired a new flavour.

Ravencrag called across from the shore, "Getting into trouble again, Sal? You remember that bottle of wasps I talked about? Sound to me like I was being optimistic." The phantasmacist had dropped his trousers and stood there in his underpants, his scrawny, white legs on display, while he tried to inspect the injury to his rear.

"How's your arse, Laccus?"

"Covered," the little man replied. "Unlike yours."

Greene sighed with resignation. Here he was helping to free a demon which, upon its release, would undoubtedly find eternities of pain for him to endure—just because he'd plucked out a few eyes and kicked it in the teeth. It probably didn't help that he had no way of paying the bastard's ludicrous summoning fee in the first place, or that the demon's own servant was equally furious with him. Cope might end up quarrelling with his undying master for the right to do wicked things to the prospector's spilled innards.

And all this to try to save his family from the curse of an angel who would certainly slay him if he failed.

1012, Greene thought, was not turning out to be best year for him.

"Fuck it," he said. Time was running out.

He kicked the sword again, then again and again, pummelling his boot against the lower edge of the grip. The steel roots snapped somewhere below the pommel, and the sword fell to the ground.

"Alright," he said, breathing hard. "Now I kicked your master's tooth out. Ask him nicely to get us out of here."

TWO BUILDINGS OF NOTE faced each other from either end of Lye Street. To the south, rose the brick tower containing the ash vats which had given the road its name. Opposite this, at the top of a rise, Barraby's Watchtower looked out across an abandoned cannon foundry, built after the Skirmishes in 880. The Church had constructed the watchtower in the seventh century. It stood in a circle of floating flagstones, pinned to its foundations by a radial arrangement of chains.

Scrimlock set the street plans down on the desk and glanced up at the sapper seated opposite. "You think she'll head for the lye tower?"

"Without a doubt, Your Grace." The woman was small but heavy-set, with a wide brow, flat nose, and masculine shoulders. She wore a faded brown jerkin and fingerless leather gloves. "It's the only uninhabited building in the street. It's high and gives a good view of the surroundings."

"Can we rig it with blackcake?"

The sapper shook her head. "Not much point, Your Grace. The walls are old, the brick crumbly, and the roof is just wood and slate. If we brought the lot down on top of her, she'd probably just shuck it off. She's torn clean through stronger buildings before."

The Presbyter clucked his teeth. Scar Night was still two days away. "Have you had a chance to survey the rest of the area?"

"As much as we can. We're moving under the street so as not to draw too much attention." She leaned forward, studied the blueprints, and prodded a finger at one section. "Our best chance to trap her is Barraby's Watchtower. The walls are built of Blackthrone stone and the windows are too narrow for her wings. If we can get her inside, we ought to be able to fix it so she can't get out again. We'll prime the roof to blow on ten yard fuses, enough to cut off her escape but keep the structure intact."

"Hmm. I want the watchtower door strengthened."

"It's iron-banded oak," the sapper said. "They designed it to keep an army out. But we'll bring in a portable buttress in the night, just to be sure. Four knocks with a hammer and it's in place."

The Presbyter nodded. "Good." .

All they had to do was lure her inside. He unravelled the scroll Merryweather had brought him and reread the information the Adjunct had gleaned from Deepgate's census, tax, and crime records.

Sal Greene, prospector, made his fortune in the Northern Deadsands, inherited 34 Lye Street from his father, Mack Greene in the 962nd Year of Our Lord Ulcis.

Minor infringements:

963-3: Reprimanded. Suspected instigator of a brawl in the Skewered Goat Inn, Callow.
963-4: Fined after a second brawl, the Skewered Goat Inn, Callow.

964-10: Fined for lewd comments made toward Agatha Constance of 13 Potter's Wheel House, Applecross.

964-10: Fined for throwing eggs at the windows of 13 Potter's Wheel House, Applecross.

964-11: Jailed for two days for stealing flowers from the garden of M. Caldershot of Lilley. Flowers subsequently discovered in the window box of a Miss Celia Norman of Applecross. Suspect confessed to charges. Recorded as telling the city militia to "Go fuck themselves sideways."

988-1: Jailed for sixty days for urinating against a monument to Ulcis in Seven Chain Square. Subject deemed unsuitable for tempering due to arthritis in hands.

Other:

980-7: Suspected of withholding tax. Unproved.

990-6: Accused of murder. Unproved.

1012-3: Suspected of smuggling heathen totems. Investigation suspended, pending additional funds.

Scrimlock pursed his lips. So this was Carnival's next intended victim? This foul-mouthed criminal and blasphemer from the Warrens was the direct descendant of Henry Bucklestrappe? The Presbyter set down the scroll and smiled to himself. He ought to be able to kill two birds with one vigorous explosion.

R UBY'S DRESSING ROOM abutted the study. It was a
small chamber with one window, shuttered to keep out
the night, and it was empty of furniture except for a stool, a tin
basin, and a white dresser with an oval mirror.

She filled the basin with hot water and washed the angel's hair.

Carnival endured Ruby's ministrations with closed eyes and
a thumping heart. She crouched over the basin, trembling each
time the old lady's fingers touched her scalp, shivering when
warm water sluiced over her neck.

Ruby hummed as she worked, and made occasional comments: "That's much better, dear," and, "You have such lovely hair
under all that grime."

There was a lot of grime. The witch changed the water three
times before she was satisfied.

Next the old lady took a brush from her dresser and teased
the knots from the angel's wet hair. This took some time, for
there were a lot of knots. After she had finished, she stepped
back to admire her handiwork.

"That will do, I think. Now let's see about those scars."

Carnival's fear and confusion returned. Hair dripping, she
backed away towards the door.

Ruby gave her a tut-tut of disapproval. "If only your poor

mother could see what a mess you've made of your pretty face," she said primly. "Still, a little liquid smoke and make-up conceals all manner of sins."

Carnival swallowed. "You knew her?" she said in a cracked voice.

"Your mother, dear, was my sister, which makes you my niece and me your aunt."

Carnival didn't know what to say. Her thoughts spun. She had *family* among these mortals, among those she preyed upon? A wave of distress rose within her. It was a lie. It had to be a lie. The scrawled messages came back to her.

LYE STREET. LIE STREET.

"You look just as shocked every time I tell you," said Ruby. "And why should you be? Why shouldn't your mother be a mortal woman? Mortal women bear the temple archons, after all."

"And my father?"

Ruby glanced away. "Well…" she said. "Let's not concern ourselves with your father right now. All in good time, dear." She opened a dresser drawer and took out a number of small pots, jars, and colourful sticks, fussing over them nervously. "Clean hair is all very well, but if you're going to look like a proper noblewoman's daughter, I'll have to work a miracle. Sit down, for goodness' sake."

She chose a pale powder which she said was made from Hollowhill lead, wood ashes, ox fat, and a handful of secret ingredients. She applied it to the scars on Carnival's face and arms with a small pad. And Carnival allowed her to. All manner of strange feelings tumbled through the angel's heart, but she sat quietly on the stool and let the witch work her miracle.

"Now, a little red for your lips," said Ruby. "Do try not to lick it; it's made from ox blood." She smeared the stuff all over Carnival's lips.

Carnival waited while Ruby applied further powders, fragrant talcum and scents. She permitted the old lady to daub her eyelids with shades of umber, then trim her nails with small silver scissors and paint them deep red.

Finally the witch stepped back again. She studied Carnival for long moment, and then smiled. "You look almost human. Well…not human, of course; but, my goodness what a difference a little face paint and eye shadow makes. I think we're seeing the real you at last. No, no, stay where you are. Don't get up and look in the mirror just yet. I have one last gift for you. My master stroke."

She hurried back into the study.

Carnival sat alone on her stool, waiting. She looked at her hands and wrists, so pale and unmarred, the cracked nails hidden under a shiny red veneer. She wondered about the human mother she could not remember. Did she resemble that woman? Who would she see when she looked in the mirror? Her heart trembled with nervous excitement.

She heard a click.

A heavy metal grate crashed down over the door. It must have been hidden inside the walls of the townhouse. Now it blocked her escape from the room. Carnival leapt from her stool. She grabbed the bars and heaved at them. They would not shift. She turned sideways, tried to squeeze between two bars, but her wings were too large to pass through the narrow gap.

"Such a slender little thing," Ruby said wistfully from the study. "Had you been a normal girl, you might just have managed that."

Carnival rushed back across the room and threw open the shutters. There was nothing there: no window, just a plain brick wall. She smashed a fist against it, again and again.

"Temper tantrums won't change a thing, dear. You're trapped."

Carnival returned to the grate. The old lady stood on the other side, clutching a coil of red ribbon in one hand and a fist of white flowers in the other.

"I had intended you to have these," she said. "Your mother always wore flowers and ribbons in her hair. But I think you look enough of a fool without them, don't you?"

MINA HAD PUT the demon Basilis in her pram and smothered him with doll's blankets, and frilly bows, and her family of painted wooden ducks. Then she had announced that she was taking Mr Bangles and the ducks for a walk and pushed the little vehicle out of the day room.

Sal Greene could hear the squeak of wheels and his granddaughter singing in the hall outside. The dog had its teeth back, but it was still a pup. When it had tried to bite Mina, she'd only got cross and hit it with a spoon.

"What does the sword do?" he said.

Ravencrag had insisted they return to Lye Street. Greene suspected this was because the little shit was worried that his fellow phantasmacists would start to ask questions about Cope. Ellie had made them breakfast and then retired to her room to let the three men speak in private. Now they reclined in comfortable chairs before the hearth.

The thaumaturge inspected the weapon. "It is a mystery," he said. "With the branch, I had only to peer closely to be shown wonders through my master's eyes. Yet this appears to be a normal blade."

"Maybe it's unbreakable," said Greene.

"Your brutish actions in the Forest of Teeth have shown that it is not, Mr Greene. See where the metal beneath the pommel was sheared by your boot."

Ravencrag lit his pipe. "I bet it drinks souls," he said. "And sends them screaming into the demon's veins."

"A novel supposition, Mr Ravencrag," said Cope. "Why do you suppose the blade drinks souls?"

The phantasmacist exhaled a cloud of smoke. "It's a magic sword," he said. "That's the sort of thing they do."

"Have you wielded a magic sword before?"

Ravencrag grunted. "That's between me and my ex-wife."

Cope studied the sword, turning it over in his hands. "I fear you are mistaken, Mr Ravencrag. I sense nothing of my master's thirst in this steel. In fact, I can discern little of him except his grim determination to kill and maim, the predilection you felt expressed by the gale in the Forest of Teeth."

"Maybe that's it," said Greene. "The blade gives the wielder some sort of unnatural skill at swordplay? Or heightened aggression?"

"Hmm." Cope looked doubtful. "I do not feel overly aggressive. But at least we can test this theory without bloodshed. Which of you will spar with me?"

"Fling it over," said Greene. "I swung a sword in my youth. I was never much good at it, mind you, but I'll fight you if you promise not to go for my bloody knees and stop when I yell."

"If you don't mind, I'd rather hold on to it," said Cope. He unsheathed the gut-sticker from his walking stick and presented it to the other man. "Will this weapon suffice?"

"Whatever you like," said Greene.

The two men faced each other in the centre of the day room. Greene lunged first. Cope parried and retorted. The sound of clashing steel continued for several minutes, until it became clear that neither man possessed a greater degree of skill than the other. They were both mediocre swordsmen.

Breathless, Greene returned to his seat. "Maybe it's just a plain sword," he said. "Or maybe it has some use in the next forest."

Cope looked up suddenly. "Of course!" he said. "The branch led us to the sword, but we lacked the means to free the weapon without violence. Basilis has now gifted us with a blade. We must journey at once to the Forest of War."

"What?" snapped Ravencrag. "Now?"

"Why not?" said the thaumaturge. "I see no sense in delaying."

But Greene objected. "Before we go cavorting through another onc of these forests," he said, "I want to get a few things settled. I hired you to kill an angel, and now it seems to me we've been sidetracked. What started as a ritual to speak to your master has become a fucking quest to set him free.

"Now…you've already made it cleat that Basilis hates me, for pulling out a few of his eyes and so on." He made a dismissive gesture. "So I want some kind of reassurance that the pair of you are going to do what you're supposed to do. I want the angel dead. I've got my family to think of."

"I am a man of honour, Mr Greene," said Cope. "And I have no intention of reneging on our deal. Basilis's imminent release is merely an unexpected bonus. In fact, I have already used my master's vision to work on your problem."

"You have? What's the plan?"

Cope nodded. "Very well, Mr Greene." He slipped the branch from the Forest of Eyes from one of his deep pockets. The branch blinked in places, and its gazes travelled the room from floor to ceiling. "Basilis has shown me much through this," he said. "Carnival is a tormented creature."

Ravencrag snorted. "You needed a fucking magic branch to tell you that?"

Cope went on, "She does not know who she is, and she cannot accept what she is. Each Scar Night, her thirst overcomes her, driving her to kill. However, this darkmoon is different because we know who the victim is likely to be." He paused.

"The Church has also learned of her vendetta against your family, Mr Greene. The Presbyter is planning to use it to his advantage."

"It won't help," said Greene. "She cuts through Spine assassins like a hot wire through cheese. And I've never seen eye to eye with that cassocked bastard or his priests in the temple. God-botherers, the lot of them. That's why I looked you up in the first place. The Church never saved my father or his father before him."

"The angel does not recall those murders," said Cope. "And yet some part of her psyche remembers Henry Bucklestrappe's crime five hundred years ago. This dark element of Carnival's personality attempts to communicate with the angel by scrawling messages on the walls of places she frequents. Carnival is unaware that she is writing the messages herself."

"You're saying she's fucked-up mad, then?" asked Ravencrag.

"Quite insane," agreed Cope. "I believe it is a result of her overwhelming need to suppress trauma in her past. She fears the messages and flees from them, but they will inevitably lead her to Mr Greene, and eventually to his descendants."

"How do we stop her?" asked Greene.

Cope leaned back in his chair. "I think I have given you enough, Mr Greene. We have the means to locate Carnival when the time comes and a weapon which may prove useful against her. Now all that remains is to release the sword's owner." He took the skull of the last hound from his travel bag and set it on his lap. "Let us begin, gentlemen."

"**M**Y BIRDS GAVE ME the idea," said Ruby. "For the make-up, I mean. I thought the charade might appeal to you."

Carnival's fists tightened around the bars of her prison. Dawn had come outside her cell; she could feel it in her howling blood, in the creaking chains around the house. The coming night would be the last before darkmoon.

"But you never submitted until tonight," the witch went on. "You always fled before I could tempt you into my cage." She toyed with the ribbon in her hand. "Year after year after year, you'd come whenever the wind made my crystal garden sing, but you wouldn't stay." She gave a small shrug. "Over the centuries I got to know you quite well, dear, although you never did remember me."

"Liar."

"Tush. A couple of half-truths here and there, perhaps. My only real lie was the claim that I could make you beautiful." Her violet eyes were smiling. "Not even I can do that, child."

Carnival said nothing.

"Shall we have that tea now?" Ruby said cheerfully.

She placed the kettle over the fire, then left the room while it warmed, returning a few minutes later with a porcelain pot and a two cups on a tray. She moved out of sight.

Carnival slumped to the ground.

The witch was fussing about at her desk, humming to herself, clinking crockery. "You brought such shame upon our family. Upon *Him*! The Church can ignore a witch when it suits them…but you? No, you can't be tolerated. Not even by yourself." She appeared before the bars again, stirring her tea with a small black key. "Would you like a cup, dear?"

Carnival knew it would be poisoned.

Ruby said, "I nearly caught you in…When was it? The sixth century. That's right…when you weren't quite so inhuman. You asked me your mother's name." She took a sip of tea. "But it would have been improper to tell you. Some part of that scarred brain of yours might remember, and I believe we should retain a little of our dead, not just from God, but from demons too. Are you sure you won't have a cup?"

The angel studied the bars of her prison—too thick to bend, too narrow for her wings to pass through the gaps between. She wandered around the cell, looking at the floor, ceiling and walls.

All brick.

The witch sipped her tea again. "I think you ought to look at yourself in the mirror," she said. "You might be pleasantly surprised."

Carnival could feel her scars throbbing under the make-up on her face, her blood tearing through her veins. The dressing table stood to one side of the grate, the mirror angled away from her.

She turned it towards her.

The face which looked back was a mask of waxy paint, as white as a Spine assassin's or a skull. It had dark, murderous eyes outlined by vulgar smears of brown paint, which had run and made streaks across its cheeks. The lips were blood-coloured and thickly distorted, the corners blurred into a hideous, lunatic grimace.

She let out a wail of anguish.

"My my," said Ruby.

The angel smashed the mirror with her fist. She kicked the dressing table savagely, reducing it to shards of wood. She fell to her knees and beat at the broken pieces with both clenched hands.

Ruby set down her cup. "I'll leave you now," she said, "and let you ponder all of this."

Carnival threw herself at the grate, clawing at the air through the bars, but the witch just smiled and said, "Let me know when you're ready for some tea, dear."

Carnival slunk back, hissing. She twisted round and round. And then she punched the wall, hard. Crumbs of brickwork fell to the floor. She gnashed her teeth, flexed her shoulders, and flung open her wings. Again she drove her fist into the wall and again and again and again. More fragments of brick crumbled.

Ruby's violet eyes shone with amusement.

The angel paused, sucking air through her teeth, feeling every fibre of her hatred twist inside her.

Then she attacked her prison. She pummelled and clawed at the brickwork. Her nails broke. She saw flashes of blood, dust, grit. Her knuckles and fingers shattered, but she ignored the pain. Fury crowded everything from her sight but the bricks before her and the frenzied blur of her fists.

Through the choking air she glimpsed sunlight.

She had made an opening.

She pushed a hand through, grabbed the edge of a brick and heaved. Rubble crashed to the floor, billowing out thicker clouds of dust. The hole had widened. Carnival kicked at the surrounding bricks. A window-sized section of the wall fell away. Sunshine flooded in, blinding her.

The witch coughed. "Dear me," she said, nonchalantly.

For a moment, Carnival could see nothing but a blaze of white light streaming through the dust. She screwed her eyes shut and reached through the hole in the wall she'd made. Her fingers closed around a metal bar.

The room had been built inside a cage.

Ruby was still coughing. "I'm sorry, dear," she said. "But I became aware of your penchant for demolition a long time ago. The temple sappers were kind enough to reinforce my dressing room for me. Both the cage and its locks are made of sapperbane, quite strong enough to hold you for all eternity."

Through her black rage, Carnival sought the source of the voice. She couldn't see anything through the roiling clouds, yet the witch sounded nearer than she had been a moment before.

How close was Ruby to the cell door?

The angel held her breath, and then reached around behind her own shoulder. Her fingers touched hard muscle, tendons, feathers. She felt for the place where her wing sprouted from her back. Then she gripped the bone and broke it.

Blind and snarling, she charged at the place where the voice had been. Her shoulders slammed against metal. The grate? She cried out in pain. Twisting, she forced herself between the bars, her broken wing hanging loosely behind her back. Agony tore through her chest. She felt ribs snap. She pushed harder. Lacking the strength to break her cage, she had broken herself instead.

Carnival would heal.

The angel groped around her. Her fingers brushed the witch's wrist.

She grabbed it.

Ruby screamed.

Carnival put her boot against the iron bars and pulled. She felt the old woman's shoulder dislocate. Then she heard a snap, fabric ripping, followed by a softer, rending sound. Warm liquid spattered her face. Still the witch shrieked and gibbered. Carnival reached back through the grate. She groped the wet floorboards until she found a stockinged foot. It tried to struggle, pull away from her, but Carnival held on firmly.

SNOW LAY THICKLY over the forest of the third hound. The trees seemed even older and more twisted here, furred with hoarfrost. Overhead, naked branches crosshatched a delicate white sky. Sal Greene's boots creaked as he walked ahead of his two companions.

"You seem much keener than before to reach my master's domain, Mr Greene."

"No point mucking around," the prospector replied. "If we're going to find the heart of the beast, let's find the fucking thing. I only hope the bastard isn't as fussy as he was the last time. Clock's ticking, Cope."

Even Ravencrag seemed to have resigned himself to Greene's determination. He kept pace with the other men, although his scowl looked like it could have pickled cabbage.

They walked for several minutes before Greene became aware of a crimson glow in the forest ahead. A mist? He sniffed the air, and a feeling of sickness crept over him.

Cope said, "The Forest of—"

"I know," Greene snapped. "I know what it is."

It was a forest of corpse trees. Like the edge of a shore, the snow ended and a land of blood began. Ahead of them, the ground glistened red. Trees of bone and flesh grew from this mire, all gangrenous and rotten. Every bole and bough bore a wound of some description, as though the trees had been set upon by an army of butchers. The whole forest was bleeding.

Ravencrag's stomach bucked.

"*This* is heart of the demon?" said Greene.

The thaumaturge's eyes were wide with wonder. "The strongest aspect of Basilis to survive intact," he confirmed. "This is the heart of Ayen's Lord of Warfare. Is it not glorious?"

To a carrion crow, perhaps. The prospector left his thought unvoiced. He did not want to converse any further with Othniel Cope.

"I can't do it." Ravencrag spat and wiped his mouth. "Gods help me, Sal, don't make me go in there."

"What did you fucking expect?" snarled Greene. "Daisies?"

The phantasmacist heaved again.

Greene growled and cricked his neck. "You and me, then, Cope." He set off into the crimson woodland.

They marched through red mulch until their boots were sodden. The ground rose and soon became treacherously slippery. To Greene's disgust, he was forced to clutch at flesh and bones in order scramble up the worst of it. Maggots infested the roots. Ribbons of fluid trickled and gurgled all around him. The stench numbed his senses.

Cope seemed unaffected by the forest; indeed, the thaumaturge appeared to delight in the wonders around him. With passion, he said, "Basilis will steer us, as he did in the Forest of Teeth."

"Steer us to what?"

"To the part of him he wishes us to retrieve."

Greene decided he'd rather not know. Unease crawled over his skin. If this rancid woodland represented the heart of Basilis, how could he, in good conscience, set the foul thing free? He thought of Cope's dog, that mangy, defenceless pup they'd left in Mina's care. The branch had granted the mutt vision. The sword had given it teeth. Yet this last forest was a place of muscle and bone. What monstrous thing would Mina's pet become?

Finally the slope levelled. They crested a ridge from where the prospector could gaze far across the landscape ahead.

Red trees stretched to the horizon under a white sky. The forest glittered like a sea of rubies. In the far distance, phantasms swooped and glided on translucent wings, their torsos scintillating gold as though clad in brilliant armour. Angels? They flocked around ivory-coloured hillocks which rose in places between the trees.

Greene halted, panting, driven to despair by this hellish vision. His topcoat hem and sleeves were greasy, clotted with scraps of gore. Liquid sloshed within his boots. He felt something wriggling between his toes.

Othniel Cope made an observation: "My master's pets have been busy making nests."

"The flying things?"

The thaumaturge nodded. "Once they were memories of warriors who attended Ayen's court, but they have since become something else. Basilis has long forgotten Heaven."

Greene continued to survey the landscape. "How far does the forest stretch?"

"It goes on forever, Mr Greene."

"Then I need a break. Forever is a long fucking way."

They rested under the boughs of a gigantic corpse tree. Sap trickled from a score of puncture wounds and other lesions, gathering in hollows between the roots. Four yards above the ground a deep gash had split the trunk open, revealing corrugated muscles, and three white, rib-like protrusions. Greene leaned against the tree, but recoiled when the bark trembled. He heard insects crawling inside.

By the time they set off again, the prospector felt even wearier than before. They moved downhill, into the vast wet woodland. With no sun to keep them travelling in a constant direction, Cope consulted his branch frequently, making alterations to their route when necessary. For a while they followed the course of a stinking brook in which white nodules floated, fording it eventually where it widened and became shallow.

Later, Greene saw a ghostly figure watching them from among the trees. He grabbed the thaumaturge and gesticulated toward the apparition.

"It's dead," said Cope. "The dead have no power here."

"I wish Ravencrag was here to see it."

"Instead of you?"

"Naturally."

The sky darkened; gloom crept into the Forest of War. The phantasms appeared more frequently, but they never moved, simply stood in silence and watched the two travellers pass by. Greene's revulsion did not waver. Each footstep he took was one too many. His instincts rejected this weird place: the sky which was not sky, the smell of the red trees, and the suck and slurp of the morass under his boots.

Finally, the thaumaturge urged him to stop. They had reached the edge of another clearing, somewhat brighter than the surrounding woodland. Narrow vein-like roots radiated from the centre, where, like some hideous tuber, grew a beating heart.

Cope brought out the sword from the Forest of Teeth and then crouched to inspect the roots. After a long moment he frowned. "This is extremely complex. I shall have to make many delicate cuts. It seems that the heart is fed by the entire forest."

"Let me," said Greene. He reached for the sword.

The thaumaturge shook his head. "You have already injured my master enough."

Greene sighed. "Suit yourself. But I reckon it's going to hurt whichever way we do it. I'm of the school which thinks it's better to get the pain over with quick, rather than suffer prolonged agony. But that's just me. Basilis might prefer his veins to be severed nice and slow."

Cope swallowed.

"Let me just stand back a yard or two," added Greene. "I don't want to be in the way when the spurting starts."

The thaumaturge's face had paled. He stared at the sword and then at the network of red roots spreading across the ground. "Perhaps you're right, Mr Greene," he said. "After all, your blunt approach has already freed two of my master's aspects. I wouldn't want to cause Basilis any unnecessary pain."

The prospector held out his hand.

Cope handed him the sword.

Green killed the man with a thrust to the back of his neck. The thaumaturge's body toppled forward to the ground.

"Sorry, Cope," muttered the prospector. "In a fair fight, you might've beaten me. I've got my family to think of."

He'd weighed it up all the way through the long trek through the Forest of War. To kill Carnival, he'd have to release Basilis. But why replace one monster with another?

And now he had little Mina to think of. Basilis would

remember his humiliation at the hands of the Greene's granddaughter.

The penultimate Scar Night of the year was due, and the old man had come to accept that he would probably die. But Ellie still had fifty years to sell the house in Lye Street and leave town. They could start a new life in Sanpah or Clune. At least there they'd have a future.

He wiped the blade clean on Cope's topcoat, then strode towards the beating heart of Ayen's Lord of Warfare. All around, ghostly figures had appeared among the corpse trees, hundreds of them. They looked on in silence.

The old prospector raised his sword above the heart. "Time to die, dog fucker."

Whirling smoke claimed him before the blade fell.

As the afternoon before Scar Night drew on, the city tensed. Labourers, eager to finish their work by sunset, bustled through Deepgate's crooked lanes with hoppers of stone, iron, and aggregate for the ongoing construction and expansion of the Warrens. Smiths worked harder at their forges. Priests rushed from home to home with their census books, and merchants chose to leave early for the River Towns.

People became edgy.

More brawls than usual broke out. In the League of Rope, the tinkers and scroungers faced increased persecution. There was a small riot and one serious house fire which claimed the lives of an elderly man and a goat.

The Tooth arrived, loaded with Blackthrone rock and mortar for the temple's new Rookery Spire. The great machine loomed above the edge of the abyss, its funnels disgorging black smoke into the heavens, reminding the faithful of the power of God.

When night fell, Carnival went to Lye Street.

Since she'd rubbed off the witch's paint, a sense of calm had come over her. She no longer feared what she might find.

A gaping window admitted her to the top of the lye tower. It was a cramped room with dead bees on the floorboards. A skeleton lay on a mat in the corner: the remains of a woman, still wearing an old-fashioned brown frock. Someone had left flowers around the body. Ash from the lye vats below covered everything in a grey veneer. A number had been scrawled on the wall opposite.

510

A doorway opened into an inner hall which led to three more rooms. Carnival wandered into the first of these.

This chamber was identical in size and layout to the first. Fragments of a smashed mirror had been strewn across the floor. The lack of ash on the glass made the angel think it had been broken recently. She saw a name scrawled on the wall.

Henry Bucklestrappe

Carnival walked back out and entered the second room: another chamber, similar to the first two. On this wall, somebody had written a second name in chalk.

Flora Whitten.

Fragments of chalk still lay on the floor beneath it. Carnival picked up a piece of it and copied the name, *Flora*, writing it underneath the first one. The handwriting matched. She had always known it would. She let the chalk fall to the floor.

In the last room she found a single word, written in her own hand.

Rape.

A small diary had been left for her on the window ledge. Carnival picked it up. It was ancient, mould-speckled, with a tarnished silver clasp. The leather bindings were falling apart, the pages brittle and yellow. She held the diary to her chest and peered out of the window. From the base of the lye tower, the street rose to the temple watchtower at the opposite end. Carnival could see the silhouettes of winged statues, falcons, perched on the building's summit, and the outline of a ballista. A Spine assassin patrolled the spaces between, nursing a crossbow in the crook of his arm.

The cobbles below glimmered faintly in the starlight, but the tenements on either side of the street were dark and shuttered, heavily barricaded against Scar Night. Deepgate remained silent, but for the distant sound of creaking chains

Carnival opened the diary and began to read.

DARKMOON HAD RISEN by the time Carnival closed
Flora Whitten's diary. She wondered why the girl had
chosen to use a rope instead of a knife in the end. So as not to
spill any blood?

To ensure she'd go to Heaven?

The angel slipped the small book into a pocket in her leather
jerkin. It fitted snugly, as though it had worn a space for itself
over many, many years. Had Carnival always carried the book
with her?

She gazed out across the dark city rooftops.

How many more secrets had she hidden from herself?
What part of her had always known the truth about Henry
Bucklestrappe's crime, had made him a promise, and then strived to
keep it all these years? Carnival must have watched and persecuted
his family for generations. It seemed to her that she harboured
a ghost inside, the shadow of a murderer who had stolen her
memories and who roamed the city while the angel slept.

She was a stranger to herself.

Now here she was in Lye Street, ready to kill a man she
didn't know.

She pulled out her knife and studied the hilt, the circle
marking she had drawn on so many walls throughout the city.

Then she brought out the crumpled flowers and ribbons she'd taken from the witch. For a long moment she looked at what she held in each scarred hand.

I can make all that is ugly about you beautiful.

Carnival threw the knife away, and heard it skitter across the rooftops. Then she tied the flowers and ribbons into her hair.

SOMEONE WAS HAMMERING on the door. It being Scar
Night, Sal Greene decided not to answer it. He wasn't that
dumb. Instead, he remained exactly where he was under the
upturned bathtub and hugged Ellie and Mina closer to his chest.

The pup yowled.

Mina nuzzled it and giggled.

A male voice shouted up from the street outside. "Open up,
citizen. Presbyter Scrimlock's orders."

Scrimlock's orders? Greene lifted the bathtub.

"Dad?"

"Stay here, princess; look after Mina. I'll just be a minute."

He padded down the stairs and unbolted the door.

Six Spine assassins stood in the street outside, their pale, wasted
faces like those of corpses. Was this about the smuggling investigation? The bastards picked a fine night to batter on his door.

Greene shot a wary glance at the old lye tower beside his house,
alert for wings, before he returned his attention to the assassins.
"If you're looking for the House of Fans," he said, "you've come
three streets too far." He pointed up the hill. "What you need to
do is go back up Lye Street, left at the watchtower—"

One of the assassins interrupted him. "We are not searching
for a brothel, Mr Greene." She had the same dull, vaporous eyes

as the others. Scrapes in her leathers indicated heavy use. "You are required to come with us for your own safety."

So Cope had been right. The Church knew all about the angel's curse.

And they thought a nice conversation under the darkmoon would be a good way to start ensuring his safety?

"Thanks but I'll pass." Greene closed the door.

He managed to get ten steps down the hallway before they broke it down.

FROM THE LYE TOWER window, Carnival watched the six temple assassins drag Sal Greene up Lye Street towards Barraby's watchtower. The sound of thumping blood rose in her ears and soon drowned out his curses. She could smell the building around her, the stench of ash and rainwater and brick. A sudden, sharp pain in her fist made her gasp. She was clutching a shard of broken mirror in her bloodied fingers. Dark, terrible eyes peered back at her from the glass. She did not recognise the face in the reflection. She stifled a scream.

Was this insanity?

Carnival met that gaze for as long as she could bear, then flung the piece of mirror away and heard it shatter against the wall.

She sucked in a deep breath and another. And then she concentrated, squeezing the window ledge until the sound of howling faded from her veins.

Quickly, she climbed through a hatch in the floor, down a ladder into the dark belly of the tower. Huge vats loomed under a canopy of rusted pipes. Water dripped, striking eerie, soulless notes in the gloom, like the heartbeat of the building itself. Beside the vats lay a massive stone trough full of brown liquid.

Carnival slid Flora's diary into the caustic solution and watched it sink from sight.

She left through the front door.

A series of blows punched air from her lungs, pitching her backwards. She crashed against the door frame, the impact jarring her newly healed wing. When she opened her eyes, she saw the shafts of bolts protruding from her chest. Carnival hissed and tore them out. Bloodied crescent metal tips clattered against the cobbles.

She looked up.

Temple assassins swarmed over the rooftops on both sides of the street, more Spine than she'd ever seen together before. She heard the click of crossbow latches, the squeal of windlass coils being rewound.

She took to the air, lashing her wings, dragging herself skywards. Skirting laundry lines, she came level with the tenement roofs. The Spine loosed their weapons again.

The impacts spun her around in the air. Lye Street reeled, and suddenly she was falling. Her foot snagged one of the laundry lines, which stretched and snapped. She hit the ground and rolled, both wings buckling under her. Her head struck something hard, metallic. A plate bolted to the street? For a heartbeat her thoughts reeled in confusion.

Where was she? Why had she come here?

From the rooftops came the sound of windlasses, the creak of laths and bowstrings drawn taught.

Carnival remembered.

Snarling, the angel leapt upright. The wounds in her chest burned as they healed. She sensed the blood clot and swell up inside her again, coursing through her veins with fresh vigour. Her dark eyes thinned. Scars itched and flared on her arms, her fists, her face.

Her knife! Where was her knife?

A cry came from the watchtower at the top of Lye Street.

Carnival spun to see a group of assassins bundling a man through the tower doorway. Their glances met. His eyes widened in fear. She recognised him. Fury bucked inside her. But then the door boomed shut, and he was gone.

Bolts whined and shattered all around her, striking the cobbles, ripping holes through her wings. Carnival roared and spat blood. Her scars writhed, tightening around her chest and neck. A shaft punctured the back of her shin. She stumbled, cried out, then yanked it out and turned and ran.

Barraby's watchtower stood pinned within a thicket of chains, all radiating outwards like a child's drawing of sunbeams. Windows gaped in its walls, as black and empty as the abyss below the courtyard foundations, yet as thin as murderholes. The door looked heavily reinforced, impenetrable. It offered her no escape from the onslaught. Carnival took to the air again as a third barrage of projectiles struck the ground behind her, driving her closer to the watchtower.

Two Spine were working furiously on the summit of the tall building, cranking an old lye ballista around on its cogged pivot, trying to bring it to bear on the angel. She tore out their throats with her hands and flung the corpses over the parapet.

Missiles whizzed over her head, the crescent tips flashing. She ducked, searching for cover. On the rooftops on either side of the street, the temple assassins surged closer, a dark wave of them. *So many!*

Then she saw the hatch in the tower roof.

She threw it open and plunged through.

She was in a dim stone chamber without windows. Against the outer wall, a curved stairwell sunk through the floor into deeper gloom. The rest of the space had been filled with clay pots, stacked one upon the other.

Carnival listened hard, hearing nothing, then stole down the stairwell.

Darkness filled the narrow space, yet the angel moved easily down the worn steps, her feathers brushing the roughcast wall. She passed a murderhole and peered out, but the narrow gap looked out upon the rear of the courtyard. She saw nothing but rusted chains, and the smokestacks of a foundry looming behind.

A hissing, crackling sound came from above. Glancing back up the stairwell, the angel spied a quiver of odd white light.

Her instincts saved her. That uncanny wiring of nerves, which had so often driven her beyond the boundaries of pain and endurance, screamed at her now.

Move!

She threw herself down the steps as a massive concussion shook the building. She heard a *crack*, followed by the crash of stone and breaking timbers. The watchtower lurched. Chunks of masonry poured into the stairwell, sealing it behind her. The air fogged with dust or smoke. Grit hissed through cracks in the darkness above.

Coughing and sputtering, Carnival picked herself up.

A second blast rumbled through the tower, this time from below.

The basement?

Carnival tore down the stairwell and reached a landing. An arched portal opened into another dismal chamber, lit by a single cresset set in a wall sconce.

The man she'd come to kill stood there, gazing at a sword on the floor.

"I picked the sword up," he said wearily. "Then I came to my senses and put it back down again. I've been walking around the fucking thing for a while now, trying to figure out what to do with it." He glanced up at her. "I don't know if they let me have it because they thought I could protect myself from you, or if it's just some kind of a sick joke. You know how Spine like their little jokes?"

Carnival stepped into the room.

Sal Greene put his hands in his pockets. "They used blackcake to blow the roof," he said. "And to seal the basement too, from the sound of things. I suppose it's a trap, and I was the bait. You ever see so many assassins in one place before?"

When the angel didn't answer, he went on, "I always reckoned this night would slip by me, one way or another. I tried to have you killed, you know? For the sake of my family. Didn't do me much good." Sadness clouded his eyes. He turned away. "You suit your hair like that, all spidery and windblown…And I like the ribbons." He sighed deeply, and took an unsteady step. He was shaking. "That's not going to work with you, is it? Not a fucking chance…"

Carnival heard a scraping sound outside, followed by four loud bangs, like hammer blows.

Greene stared at the wall. "Just tell me one thing," he said. "What the fuck did Henry Bucklestrappe do to you?"

She grunted. "You don't know?"

"Honestly? No."

"To me? Nothing." She heard boots moving softly up the stairwell.

Greene shook his head and smiled sadly. "You were looking out for someone else then? Shit, I never imagined it was that." He met her eyes again. "A friend of yours?"

The angel shrugged. She could no longer remember.

The old man frowned a little, but he had a look in his eyes which might have been wry amusement. "I wasn't lying about

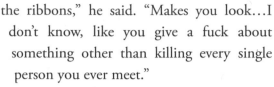

the ribbons," he said. "Makes you look…I don't know, like you give a fuck about something other than killing every single person you ever meet."

From outside the tower came the rasp of a hundred blades drawn.

Carnival felt the darkmoon thirst rise inside her, quickening her pulse, inflaming her scars. Her hands tightened into fists. She wondered what she'd done with her knife.

Behind her, the footsteps grew louder. She heard the scrape of steel against the stairwell wall. The temple assassins had almost reached her. The Spine sword lay on the floor before her, its hammered steel edges gleaming in the light of the cresset. Carnival moved to pick up the weapon, but stopped.

I can make all that is ugly about you beautiful.

The angel raised a hand to touch the ribbons and flowers she had woven into her hair, and she thought about the hellish eyes she'd seen reflected in the shard of mirror. Was that how she appeared now? Despair swamped her heart. Tears prickled the corners of her eyes.

Unarmed, she turned away to meet her enemies.

They came upon her in the landing beyond the chamber: an old assassin closely followed by three of his colleagues. His grizzled face showed no hint of fear. Sword already out, he moved as quickly and gracefully as a man of half his years.

Carnival had no intention of fighting or retreating. A feeling of numbness had filled her limbs. She did not move as the Adept thrust his blade upwards at her heart. The steel point flashed, drove deep into the angel's leather armour. She felt the metal split her flesh, the weapon's edge catch her ribs.

Pressure in her chest forced her back. Carnival tasted blood in her throat. She leaned forward into the sword and looked into her opponent's eyes. There was nothing there—no surprise or wonder at the angel's unusual actions, naught but the vacant stare of a temple assassin going about the business of murder. The Adept placed his free hand behind the sword's pommel, and pushed the blade in deeper.

The angel's heart convulsed. She gasped.

But then she felt the wound begin to heal. Refusing to suffer such punishment, the flesh beneath her tapestry of scars fought back. Carnival's heartbeats strengthened and became steady again. Blood thickened around the gash in her chest, stemming the flow. From somewhere deep inside, her rage and instincts took over.

Suddenly, without intending to, she was clutching the naked blade in one lacerated fist, pulling it back out even as her free hand shot up and grabbed the assassin's neck. She squeezed hard, crushing his windpipe and arteries, and threw him backwards into the other Spine.

The blade clattered to the floor.

Carnival screamed.

And madness took over. She set upon her foes, meeting their swords with her fists, knees, and elbows, laughing and shrieking like a demon. The Spine backed away. With her wings like a wall of darkness behind her, the angel advanced down the stairwell. She killed two, four, eight of them. She shattered bones and ripped off ears. She wept and giggled and spat blood in their faces.

The Spine had no use for crossbows in such a confined space, so they fought with swords. And they fought well. Blades flashed in the gloom before Carnival. She deflected blow after blow, driving the weapons aside. Steel clashed and sparked against the stone walls.

They were quite quick, she supposed, for mortals.

And still they came, climbing in now through the watchtower's narrow windows. They rushed down the steps behind, clambering over the bodies of the fallen, to surround her. In the narrow confines of the stairwell, they attacked from above and below.

She slaughtered them all. And when the dead blocked the passageway, she forced their broken corpses through the windows so that more of her enemies could reach her. Yet her own savagery appalled her. Blood covered her scars and dripped from her broken fingernails. Her ancient leathers bore a thousand new cuts and abrasions. Amidst her fury she suffered bouts of anguish. She cried out, begging her foes to leave her alone, and then butchered them when they refused. Abandoned weapons littered the steps, but Carnival could not bring herself to pick one up.

In time, she fought her way down to the watchtower antechamber. Vaulting over a heap of twitching corpses, she came to a heavy door. The iron-banded beams had been designed to hold back an army. She waited a heartbeat before testing her rage against it. The barrier resisted the first blow and the second.

And then the Spine reinforcements arrived.

Here the temple assassins had room to manoeuvre. Their black armour gleamed in the torchlight. They poured down the stairwell and into the antechamber. Blades arcing, they rushed to flank the angel, attacking as one. Steel flickered and hissed and cut the air around her. Carnival screamed and wove between the blows, the shadows of her wings towering behind her, until the last sword crashed to the blood-soaked floor.

She was alone.

Voices came from outside the watchtower. She heard a man praying, followed by the dull tones of another assassin. This second man said, "It's over."

Carnival flexed her shoulders and licked the blood from her lips. The antechamber reeked of violence. Torches guttered and crackled in their sconces, illuminating the wet red arcs which covered the walls. Corpses and bloody swords littered the floor.

It's over?

The angel grunted. She crouched, took a deep, snarling breath, and then threw herself at the door.

Cool night air rushed in to the sound of ruptured timbers.

Two men were outside. A Spine Adept had been thrown backwards by the force of the breaking door, but he was already rising to his feet, his sword ready. The other man wore the cassock of a priest. He was kneeling to one side of the doorway, staring at the angel in terror. "She's here," he hissed

Carnival gazed past the two men, to where the chains around Barraby's watchtower cut the night sky into countless triangles. Stars glittered among the iron, bathing the city rooftops in pale silver light.

She spied movement everywhere: the silhouettes of fifty or more temple assassins. They were scaling the chains lithely, dropping down to the courtyard below, converging on her. All Adepts? Carnival tried to force her lips into a smile, but the expression felt ugly and unnatural.

She glanced down at the kneeling priest and said, "Run."

When dawn broke, a long line of priests arrived with mops and buckets to clean up the gore around Barraby's watchtower. They lit incense burners and prayed for the lives of all the Adepts who'd been lost. No one knew exactly what had happened, or what had gone wrong. Presbyter Scrimlock, it was said, had locked himself in the temple library and would not come out.

The sudden appearance of an old man at the watchtower door was never recorded, at least not in the official account, but other writings agree that he stepped out of the building nevertheless. He wore a heavy woollen topcoat, covered in dust. When he saw the sun he lifted his chin and took a long, deep breath.

Then he strolled down Lye Street to number 34 and let himself in.

Some claimed that Sal Greene had been involved in the disappearance of a phantasmacist, a known scoundrel who had run a club in the Ivygarths district of the city, but no formal charges were ever brought to bear. Temple census documents show that he lived a long life in Deepgate without ever returning to the heathen cities he had known so well in his youth. When he finally died, his Sending was unremarkable.

His daughter Ellie became a seamstress, and was respected among the ladies of Lilley. She lived happily with her husband Jack, content to remain in Deepgate. Yet the old prospector's granddaughter, Mina, had obviously inherited something of his wanderlust.

Even as child Mina had been bold, widely known in the Warrens on account of a tiny mongrel which she pushed around in a pram. Her mother's stable employment, coupled with a weakness to pander to her daughter's whims, ensured that Mina's dog was never seen in the same frock twice. It was a foul tempered creature, always growling and trying to bite anyone who got too close. Mina admonished it constantly with the back of a spoon. The pair became a focus for gossip in the neighbourhood. So much so, that when Mina left the chained city for Sanpah in her early twenties, some even said she took with her the very same ragged little pup.